# He replied by swiftly unclasping and unzipping her skirt.

It fell to her ankles immediately, and she stepped over it.

Suddenly they were turning and touching like a pair of demented dancers, clothes falling free as they frantically kissed their way out of the sitting room.

He scooped her up into his arms.

'Giovanni—' she gasped.

His blue-black eyes glittered. 'What?'

'Where are you taking me?' As she spoke the words, she knew that it was a foolish and redundant sentence, and his abstract and almost cynical smile told her that he felt exactly the same way.

'To bed,' he ground out, as he kicked the door open.

# THE SICILIAN'S PASSION

BY
SHARON KENDRICK

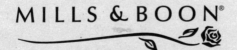
MILLS & BOON®

With special thanks to Mary D'Angelo
of the Italian Cultural Institute
and Sarah Locke (of Winchester!)
and Victoria and Alexandra and, of course, dear old Goethe.

*First published in Great Britain 2001
Harlequin Mills & Boon Limited,
Eton House, 18-24 Paradise Road, Richmond, Surrey TW9 1SR*

© Sharon Kendrick 2001

ISBN 0 263 82540 X

*Set in Times Roman 10¼ on 11½ pt.
01-1001-53835*

*Printed and bound in Spain
by Litografia Rosés, S.A., Barcelona*

# CHAPTER ONE

IT WAS probably the sexiest car Kate had ever seen. Black and sleek and gleaming, it positively *screamed* testosterone! And it looked all wrong on the forecourt of such an imposing mansion.

Kate smiled. In her experience, only dull little men drove around in cars like that—as if compensating for their own inadequacies with an excess of horsepower!

She squinted at it curiously. Lady St John, her client, was a very wealthy woman, yes—but in a restrained rather than an over-the-top way. Since when had she taken to entertaining people who owned such outrageously powerful cars?

Unless she had taken to driving one herself, thought Kate, her mouth quirking in amusement. It wouldn't surprise her.

She studied the car again. Maybe not. Lady St John had an abundance of energy—but you would need to be pretty agile to gain access to *that* long, low and mean machine!

She took one last glance in the driving mirror before she presented herself and looped back a stray strand of fiery hair. Considering that she had been up since six that morning she didn't look *too* bad! And appearances, as she knew, were everything. Particularly in her business.

Kate Connors; interior designer to the rich and—sometimes—famous. And, as jobs went, it was… Well, as she often reminded herself, it was pretty cool. It paid well, it had variety, and what was more—it enabled her to meet all kinds of interesting people.

Like Lady St John—an intrepid aristocrat who had travelled to all corners of the globe and then produced exciting—if somewhat under-read—books all about her journeys.

The St John house was as rugged as the magnificent sweep of coastline which lay to the front of it, and as Kate jangled the old-fashioned doorbell, she could hear the thunder of the sea as it crashed and foamed against the craggy grey rocks.

Such an elemental place, she thought, wishing that her job was not almost at an end, as the door was opened by the housekeeper.

'Hello, Mrs Herley,' smiled Kate. 'Lady St John is expecting me, I believe?'

The woman gave a brief smile as she pulled the door open to usher Kate inside. 'I think that your appointment may have slipped her mind,' she confided. 'Lady St John is a little…er…distracted today.'

Kate knew better than to ask why. It hadn't taken her long in the job to discover that domestic employees never gave away information about their employer—and particularly not one as naturally autocratic as the rather formidable Elisabeth St John, who was nearly eighty, and yet Kate had never met a woman of such advanced years who could exude such beauty and such grace. Who could still wear clothes with the style of the fashion model she had once briefly been. If *I* look like that at her age, she had thought at their very first meeting, then I would be a very happy bunny indeed!

Mrs Herley shut the door again. 'If you would like to wait in the Blue Drawing Room, Miss Connors, then I will tell Lady St John that you are here.'

'Thanks,' murmured Kate rather wryly.

Her early appeal to Mrs Herley that she 'call me Kate' had fallen on polite but deaf ears—and she had remained Miss Connors ever since! Some people's worlds were built on different structures from her own. But such formality suited this beautiful old house, she decided dreamily, making her way to the enormous room which she was almost through with decorating.

Kate let out a sigh as she looked around. She would be

sad to let it go—but then, that happened with nearly all her jobs. They were her babies, in a way, and the final parting always proved more of a wrench than she expected, even after nearly nine years in the business.

The floor-to-ceiling windows were filled with the image of sea and sky—a breathtaking view and one with which the room had needed to compete so that it didn't fade into complete insignificance.

Kate had chosen the colours carefully, and now the walls were bright with an unusual shade of blue. A deep and stunning and startling blue, and one which made the most of the Gothic mouldings which adorned the cornices.

And if she said so herself—it did look pretty good!

'Kate?'

She turned around to find Lady St John walking into the room, in a cashmere cardigan and matching ankle-skimming skirt.

'Hello, Lady St John! Almost my last visit to you, sadly! And I...I...' Kate's words faltered and then died completely, stuck in her throat like an insult one had thought better of saying.

For Lady St John was not alone, and insult was the very last word you would associate with the man who had quietly entered the room behind her. For who could possibly criticise pure perfection on two such long, muscular legs? This must be the owner of the car, she realised, and her heart began to race. Had she thought that only dull little men drove cars like that? Because she had been totally and foolishly wrong.

Lady St John performed a seamless introduction, waving her hand in the direction of the man who stood like a dark, silent statue behind her. 'Kate—this is my godson.'

'Your *godson*?' echoed Kate, in breathless bemusement.

Lady St John smiled. 'Mmm! I met his mother on my youthful travels to Europe and she became one of my closest friends. I'd like you to meet Giovanni Calverri.' She turned to the man at her side. 'Giovanni, this is Kate Connors, who has just been turning her rather spectacular talents to this room.'

As he glanced around the room, Kate couldn't take her eyes off him. His name implied Latin blood, as did the jet-dark hair, though the eyes were—rather disconcertingly—a bright, dazzling blue. But the term Latin implied warmth and passion, and wasn't there something awfully *cold* and aloof about this tall, striking man who was eyeing her with a face that was closed and shuttered?

She matched his look with one of her own. Men in suits that looked as if they had only just left the designer's show-room the previous day were simply not her type.

'Hello,' she said coolly.

Giovanni froze. He had never seen a woman quite so tall or so slim, nor with hair of such a bright, beaten fire—and her very unexpectedness beat a deep, inevitable path into his consciousness. He felt the muscles of his thighs clench, as if his body was instinctively telling him that he wanted to…wanted to… His mouth hardened as he acknowledged the rampant flurry of his thoughts.

He forced himself to make his introduction as bland as possible, although the moist gleam of her mouth filled him with an overwhelming urge to crush its soft pinkness beneath his.

'Giovanni?' prompted his godmother, looking at the forbidding set of his shoulders in mild perplexity.

He pulled himself together. 'I am delighted to meet you,' he said, in the most beautiful accent Kate had ever heard—rich and dark and overlaid with the slightest and sexiest transatlantic drawl.

Say that again like you meant it, thought Kate indignantly. But she didn't stop staring, because, even though he was not her type, he was still remarkable, and men who looked like this one were few and far between. Even in the rarefied circles in which she mixed.

Olive skin, an aquiline nose and a hard, sensual mouth. Combine those attributes with a body which was tall and lithe and didn't possess even the tiniest bit of excess flesh, and you had a man who was most women's fantasy come true in living, breathing form.

'Delighted to meet you, too,' she murmured, tempted to echo his own lack of enthusiasm, but good manners brought her up short and she gave him a polite smile. 'You're Italian, are you?'

'Italian?' His mouth twisted with a derision which made it look very sexy indeed, and Kate felt her heart race again. What on earth had she said to make him glare at her so?

'*Diu Mio!*' he uttered softly, a warning glitter lighting up the depths of his blue eyes, as if she had inflicted some silent blow on him. 'I am a Sicilian, not an Italian!'

He made the claim as if he owned the world itself! 'You mean there's a difference?' she questioned lightly and batted her eyelashes playfully at him.

'Oh, dear,' murmured Lady St John.

Giovanni felt his muscles tense once more as he met the flirtatious challenge which had suddenly made her eyes look very green indeed. Eyes which were almost on a level with his own. It was a new and unsettling sensation not to be looking down on a woman—from a purely physical point of view. Disturbingly, he found himself wondering how their bodies would feel if they were touching head to toe, horizontal. *Naked.* He swallowed the thought down and sublimated his desire, preferring instead to dwell on her ignorance.

'You mean you don't know the difference between Sicily and Italy?' he demanded.

'I wouldn't have to ask if I *knew*, would I?' she returned, though his rudeness was doing nothing to dampen down the heat in her blood.

Giovanni bit back his irritation, for why should this pale and unknown Englishwoman know anything about the deep, secret place which was his home? The place in love with its own silence, which shaped the impenetrable character of all Sicilians.

'The difference is almost incalculable,' he told her coldly. 'And would take far more time to explain than I have at my disposal.'

'I see,' said Kate faintly, thinking how well he spoke English—whilst at the same time acknowledging that she could not ever remember anyone being *quite* so rude to her!

'Giovanni!' said Lady St John, with a mild air of reproval. 'Much more of that severity and you'll have Kate leaving!'

He turned then, and a sudden brief flash of warmth transformed the chilly face as he looked down at his godmother. 'Forgive me,' he murmured, 'but it has been a very long week. You must make allowances for me if I am not up to giving a history of Sicily this close to lunch!'

Kate was furious. Was he going out of his way to make her feel as though she was something he had found squashed beneath the sole of his delicious, handmade shoe?

'Oh, don't worry about *me*, Lady St John,' she declared airily. 'It would take a lot more than *that* to make me cut and run!'

Giovanni observed the fire which was spitting from eyes as perfectly shaped as bay leaves. For a brief moment he wondered what it would be like to see those same eyes sleepy and satiated in the aftermath of passion, and then hardened his heart against their emerald appeal, astonished to find his body stubbornly attempting to disobey his will.

And yet he had had a lifetime's practice of seeing beautiful, intelligent women looking at him with open invitation in their eyes. It happened with such monotonous regularity that he was nothing more than bored by it. Usually.

He told himself that she was a predator—that she must put

out for every man she wanted, in just this way—and thankfully the fire began to leave his loins.

Confused, Kate turned away from that beautiful, condemning face and tried to pretend that he wasn't there. 'I have the curtains in the van, Lady St John,' she said, gleaming a small smile of pleasure at her client. 'And I'd like to begin hanging them, if I may.'

'I can't wait to see them!' enthused Lady St John. 'Shall we ask Giovanni to help you carry them in? They must be very heavy indeed.'

Ask for help from the cold-faced man who had been so rude to her? Like hell! Kate shook her head, and the red hair shimmered like a windblown wheat-field all the way down her back. 'That won't be necessary!' She gave him a defiant smile. 'I'm used to managing on my own!'

'How admirably independent!' His blue eyes mocked her as did the smile which hovered around his lips. 'But I am afraid that consideration for the weaker sex is inborn in all Sicilian men. I insist on helping you.'

Had he deliberately said that just to inflame her? The weaker sex indeed! And how could he insist against her wishes? Kate opened her mouth to snap back some suitable retort, until she realised that it wouldn't make very good business sense to be rude to her client's godson. Even if he did need a few lessons in manners! And the curtains really *were* very heavy.

'How terribly *sweet* of you,' she emphasised deliberately.

Giovanni silently registered the affront, with another stab of heat to his belly. Sweet was not a description which most red-blooded men strove for. Was she hoping to goad him into some kind of reaction, perhaps? His smile grew even colder. Women were notoriously predictable and he was in grave danger of giving her back just the response she wanted. 'Why, you are much too kind!' he murmured back.

Kate felt more than a little out of her depth as she led the way out of the house towards her van. Not a feeling she was used to—and certainly not one with which she was comfortable.

She was sunny and enthusiastic—qualities which were normally contagious. When you worked closely alongside people in their own homes, you had to get along with them. And normally she didn't have a problem getting along with anyone.

So what was the problem here? Or was Giovanni the problem?

It's not his home, she reminded herself as she pointed to her van. It belongs to his godmother. He's obviously just into all that macho stuff—maybe he thinks it turns women on. Well, she should let him know loud and clear that it didn't! 'All the stuff's in there!' she said, pointing rather frustratedly at the van.

'Yes,' he said, narrowing his eyes to look at her as she unlocked the back of a van only a little more flamboyant than she was, and began to climb inside.

She wore a pair of slim-fitting trousers in a soft green as vibrant as the newest buds of spring—stretched closely over a bottom which was high and taut. She half turned, and Giovanni swallowed as his eyes flickered over a tangerine Lycra T-shirt which clung to the lush swell of her breasts.

Most redheads would never have worn a shirt that orange, he decided. But, then, hair that thick and bright was rare indeed. It hung almost to her waist, clipped back from her pale, freckled face with two clips of glittering pink plastic which matched the bangles that jangled around her narrow wrists.

Giovanni had been brought up to believe that a woman should only ever wear gold. Or diamonds. That their bodies should only ever be clothed in silk or cashmere, or the lightest of cottons. Pure, natural fabrics to enhance feminine beauty—not these clinging, man-made clothes. He wondered if her underwear was just as garish and his mouth hardened. What in *Diu*'s name had made him think of something like *that*?

'Here we are!' said Kate breathlessly, hauling out a huge, plastic-sheathed package from the depths of the van. And then she looked up to find those cold blue eyes studying her with an intensity which was almost…almost… Her own eyes narrowed in response as she realised that the overriding expression on his face was one of censure!

What made this arrogant stranger think he had the right to look down on *her*?

She curved her lips into a smile. Be pleasant, she urged herself. Or, at least, be outwardly pleasant. Don't react. Reacting will look like a challenge and this man looked too ruthless an adversary to risk challenging.

'Think you can manage it OK?' she asked kindly.

The insincere smile was almost as insulting as her question. She was employed by his godmother, for heaven's sake—and here she was looking down that freckled snub of a nose as though he was some kind of odd-job man! Giovanni fought the desire to retaliate, even though she was just asking to be put in her place.

'Give it to me,' he instructed softly, his voice dipping in Latin caress.

And to her horror Kate found herself responding to that silky order as if he had been talking about something entirely different. She felt her senses spring into some kind of magical life—inspired by nothing more than a throwaway comment. Since when had her self-esteem been so low that she found something as derogatory as that a *turn-on*?

'Here.' She would have dumped the precious package in his arms if it hadn't been worth a small fortune. As it was she laid it there as tenderly as if it were a newborn infant, and just for a moment their hands brushed and she felt the unwelcome sizzle of longing. 'I'll bring the rest of the stuff inside,' she said, hoping that he hadn't noticed.

He had, of course. It had happened too often in his past for him not to. Desire could strike inappropriately and randomly; he accepted that. And sometimes, though not often, he was tempted as any man would be tempted—but he had never yet succumbed to the lures of fleeting desire. His sense of honour was too deeply ingrained in him to ever do that.

But Giovanni could never recall a temptation as potent as the one he was experiencing now. He turned his back on her and without another word began to walk back towards the house.

Lady St John was still in the Blue Drawing Room and she turned around with a smile as Giovanni brought the heavy package into the room and placed it on a table.

'Would you like us to leave you alone now, Kate?' she asked. 'I know you prefer to work undisturbed.'

'Oh, yes, please!' answered Kate gratefully, trying to imagine hanging heavy brocade under the scrutiny of that critical blue gaze. Why, she would probably break the habit of a lifetime and drop the curtains all over the floor!

'And afterwards you'll join us for lunch, I hope?'

Usually, of course, she did. But today? With this moody-looking godson? Thanks, but no, thanks! 'Well, it's very sweet of you, but I think I might run over time, and I'd hate to delay you—'

'No trouble at all,' said Lady St John immediately. 'Giovanni has expressed a wish to see the gardens—and I can't wait to show him how many exotic plants we have acquired in the conservatory!'

'But perhaps Miss Connors has lost her...appetite?' he murmured, and his eyes darkened in predatory challenge.

She most certainly had—and he knew it, too! Kate met a mocking blue gaze and knew that this was something she could not refuse—and when she thought about it, why ever *should* she? Why let this contemptuous individual put her off, when during every other visit she had enjoyed a congenial and delicious meal with Lady St John before setting off back to London? Surely she was accomplished enough in the ways of the world to be able to act indifferently when she wanted to?

'I haven't eaten since six this morning,' she said truthfully. 'I'd love lunch!'

Giovanni looked at her, and wondered if she was one of those women who could eat with genuine appetite and remain as slim as a blade of grass. Or would a hearty lunch mean that she would exist on nothing but water and fresh air for the next three days?

'Good! Come on, Giovanni,' said Lady St John resolutely. 'Let me show you colours that could rival your Sicilian flora!'

He gave a benign but disbelieving laugh. 'I do not think so!'

Once they had gone, Kate took out the heavy brocade curtains, and set about pinning them up, running her fingertips down their shiny pleats. When she worked she was focused, seeing nothing more than colour and texture taking shape before her eyes, and she put the dark-haired Sicilian out of her mind.

She had just finished when she heard a soft footfall behind her, and she turned on her stepladder to find Giovanni standing there, his gaze arrested by the brilliant glimmer of deep blue and gold.

And then the gaze was lifted almost reluctantly to her face, and Kate felt herself imprisoned—impaled, almost—by a shaft of blinding sapphire light.

'You look surprised,' she observed in a low voice.

He was. He had expected…what? That she was too modern, too up-to-the-minute, and that the fabric she chose would look shockingly out of place in this beautiful old house.

'A little,' he conceded, with a very Sicilian shrug of his shoulders.

'You thought I would have poor taste?'

He looked at her. She had perception, he noted. And such green eyes. And hair like fire. He felt some unknown and unwanted sensation washing over his skin. 'You should not ask questions to which you do not wish to hear the answers.'

How ridiculously old-fashioned he sounded! 'I'm a big girl, Mr Calverri—'

'*Signor* Calverri,' he corrected softly.

How could he possibly make his own name sound so beguiling? 'And?' she challenged in a husky voice she didn't quite recognise as her own. 'On the question of taste?'

He saw the quickening of her breath, and felt it fire a rapid response in his heart. 'Your taste is quite exquisite,' he said quietly.

Kate let her eyelids flutter down before he read the unwelcome hunger in her eyes. She didn't *like* him! So why did she want to keep running his compliment round and round in her head like an old-fashioned record?

'Thank you,' she said breathlessly, feeling as uncoordinated as a giraffe as she slowly stepped down off the ladder, unspeakably relieved to see his godmother appear, her face one of delight as she surveyed the finished effect.

'Oh, Kate! It's perfect!'

'You're sure?'

'Better than I could have hoped for in my wildest dreams!'

Kate found herself having some pretty wild dreams of her own—and most of them seemed to involve the unsmiling face of Giovanni Calverri, trying to imagine what it would be like to be undressed by him or to be kissed by those hard, sensuous lips.

'Why, Kate,' said Lady St John, with a little frown of concern, 'you'd better come and have some lunch—you've gone quite pale!'

'H-have I?' She touched her fingertips to her cheeks, and prayed for co-ordination to return.

The three of them walked to the light-filled room which overlooked the garden and Giovanni found his eyes being drawn to the graceful curve of her neck, feeling his senses spring into life as he told himself that she was resistible. Easily resistible. But the sunlight that flooded through the windows had made her hair look even brighter—as though someone had put a flame to it, and the waves were made of dancing fire.

He was unsmiling as he waited for the two women to sit down, and Kate thought that she had never seen a face quite so devoid of emotion. Or so compelling. And she became aware of the sudden soft rush of colour to her cheeks.

Giovanni saw her blush, and interpreted the unmistakable reason behind it, feeling his heart begin to hammer in his chest as he realised how much she wanted him.

'Have a glass of wine, Kate,' smiled Lady St John.

Kate shook her head as she tried to avoid the clash of that blue stare, the small but knowing smile which was playing at the corners of a mouth which looked almost *cruel*. Wine was the very last thing she needed. 'Just water for me, thanks—I'm driving. And I have to get back to London straight after lunch.'

What a pity, Giovanni found himself thinking and then, with a huge effort of will, pushed her green-eyed temptation to the very recesses of his mind.

It was an endurance test of a meal which Kate forced herself to eat. Because if she pushed her food round and round her plate, wouldn't he be able to tell how debilitated she felt in his presence? How aware she was of those long, olive fingers as they casually broke bread and then sensuously placed a fragment in his mouth? Why, she was in danger of acting like an overgrown schoolgirl, with a schoolgirl's crush! At twenty-seven, for heaven's sake!

She cleared her throat and forced herself to look directly at him, unprepared for another sudden, sharp tug of longing. He isn't your type, she told herself again. He isn't!

'So are you just over here for business or for…for—' she got the next word out with some difficulty '—pleasure?' she finished on a gulp.

He noted the faltering quality of her voice without surprise, the tremble of her mouth which made him long to taste its sweetness, and was appalled at his own weakness. 'Business brings me to England,' he said, his accent deepening. 'But it is always a pleasure to see my godmother.'

Kate persevered, forcing herself to continue as if he were just anyone and she was networking. 'And what is your business, exactly?'

'This!' Lady St John waved an elegant hand at the solid silver candelabra which adorned the centre of the table and at the exquisitely fashioned knives and forks they were using. 'The Calverri family exports silver all over the world,' she said proudly.

And suddenly Kate made the connection—if she hadn't been quite so reluctantly dazzled by the man she might have made it a whole lot sooner. 'Calverri silver?' she asked him faintly. 'You mean, *the* Calverri silver?'

'There *is* only one,' he told her arrogantly.

Which explained the outrageously expensive car and the outrageously expensive suit—his air of only being used to the very best. Because Calverri silver—recreating classic, antique pieces, or creating timeless new ones—was a must-have for anyone with taste and plenty of money.

'Your company is doing very well,' Kate offered.

'But of course! Under Giovanni's guiding hand, it has become truly international,' said Lady St John, with another proud smile at her godson.

He shrugged. 'We have an exemplary workforce,

Elisabeth,' he murmured. 'I am simply a small cog in a very well-oiled machine.'

Kate thought that modesty did not become him, and something in the look of challenge which he glittered across the table at her told her that he probably had a good idea *exactly* what she was thinking. She broke the stare and looked down with determination at her salmon instead. Was she going completely mad? Since when had anyone ever been able to read her mind?

'This is delicious,' she said politely.

Liar, thought Giovanni as she chewed without enthusiasm. You have barely touched a thing, *angela mia*.

The plates had just been cleared away, when her mobile phone began shrilling from her bag, and Kate stared down at it in consternation as she heard Giovanni's unmistakable click of annoyance. What had she been thinking of? She *always* switched her phone off when she was eating!

'I'm sorry,' she said, reaching down for her bag.

'The curse of technology,' came his low, mocking response.

'You'd better answer it, hadn't you?' asked Lady St John mildly.

'If you don't mind.' Kate grabbed the bag and rose to her feet. 'I'll take it outside.'

But she was happy to escape from that unsettling stare and equally unsettling presence, and even happier to discover that it was Lucy who was calling. Lucy, her beloved older sister, who worked for Kate and ran her life like clockwork.

Kate clicked on the 'talk' button. 'Lucy, hi! No, no, no, of course I understand—it can't be helped! An emergency is an emergency!'

'Kate, what on earth are you talking about?' Lucy sounded confused. '*What* emergency?'

'No, of course I can come back immediately,' babbled

Kate loudly. 'I've just finished here, and I'm sure that I can be excused pudding and coffee!'

'No doubt you'll give me some kind of explanation later,' came Lucy's dry response.

'Oh, definitely! Definitely!' breathed Kate. Though how on earth would she put into words that she had fallen for a man with a cold, contemptuous face? The most beautiful man she had ever seen? And she wanted him, this blue-eyed stranger.

She shivered as she acknowledged the awful truth.

She *wanted* Giovanni Calverri!

# CHAPTER TWO

'KATE, what on earth is the *matter* with you?'

Kate looked at her sister with an unaccustomed blankness in her eyes.

She had spent the whole drive back from Lady St John's house in Sussex veering between disbelief and self-disgust. In fact, the whole journey had been negotiated on some kind of auto-pilot. She had gone straight upstairs to Lucy's flat, and it wasn't until she was inside its elegant interior that she began shaking uncontrollably—like a person who had just come down with a fever.

'It's stupid. It's nothing.' She shook her head distractedly. 'It would sound too far-fetched to explain—'

Lucy's forehead creased with perplexity. 'But Kate, you *never* leave your phone switched on during lunch. It's one of your "unbreakable rules", remember?'

Oh, yes, she remembered all right. And another of those rules was that she didn't fall victim to grand and irrational passions. That she was ruled by her head, and not her heart. That she liked and respected herself, so that falling for a man who played the 'treat them mean and keep them keen' ticket was simply *not* on her agenda.

'I just met a man,' she said slowly, and ridiculously it sounded like the first line to a love song.

The frown disappeared, and Lucy relaxed. 'Oh! And about time, too,' she smiled, with the approval of someone who was happily established in a long-term relationship. 'I've been waiting for you to fall in love for years and years!'

Kate nodded. So had she. But love was not an appropriate word, not in this case. If she was being brutally honest—and she always tried for honesty—then wouldn't falling in *lust* be a more fitting description of what had happened to her some time over lunch?

She compressed her mouth into a determined line. 'It isn't like that,' she insisted. 'I don't love him. How can I when I barely know him?'

'But Cupid's arrow has hit you with unfailing accuracy?'

'A thunderbolt,' admitted Kate in a dazed kind of voice. 'The kind of thing you read about but think will never happen to you.'

'Yes, I know.' Lucy gave a wistful smile. 'The French call it a *coup de foudre*.'

Kate shook her head. 'That would imply that it was mutual.'

'And wasn't it?'

Kate thought about it. There had been an undeniable fizzle between them, yes, but...but... 'He looked at me as though he didn't really like what he saw.'

'Or what he *felt* perhaps,' said Lucy perceptively.

Kate looked at her sister. Two years older and the most beautiful woman she had ever seen, with her dark copper hair and thick-fringed green eyes.

Lucy had been born with looks to burn and a certain irresistibility to the opposite sex. But in the end she had fallen for her boss, unwilling and unable to stop the relationship even when the powers-that-be had threatened her with the sack if she did not.

Lucy had duly lost her job, and although Jack had not he had left anyway, using the opportunity to work for himself at long last. But at least they had stayed together, thought Kate, even if Jack now spent the majority of his life abroad. And Kate had been able to offer her sister a job as her assistant at just the right time. That was the pay-off for being neighbours as well as workmates, she realised. As sisters, she and Lucy looked out for one another.

She looked around Lucy's flat, which, with Jack helping to pay for it, was much larger and more opulent than her own.

'How's things?' she asked absently, still unable to get Giovanni out of her head.

Lucy stared at her. 'Tell me about him,' she said suddenly. 'This man who's making you tremble like that.'

Kate looked down with surprise at her unsteady hands. What could she say? That he had the coldest, proudest and most beautiful face she had ever seen? And eyes so startlingly blue that the summer sky would have paled in comparison? She shrugged, but her shoulders felt unusually heavy. 'There's nothing to tell. Like I said, I don't know him. I've barely exchanged half a dozen words with him. He's Lady St John's godson—'

'Mmm. So, he's well-connected, then?' murmured Lucy.

'Oh, yes. And he's Italian—or, rather, he's Sicilian.'

'There's a difference?'

'That's exactly what I said! And apparently there is. A huge difference.' Kate thought of his quietly furious response to her innocent question. 'His family owns the Calverri silver factory. You must have heard of them.'

Lucy's eyes widened. 'You *are* kidding?'

'No, I'm not. He's rich. He's handsome.' Kate shut her eyes and forced herself to see facts rather than fantasy. He is curiously unsmiling and there is an impenetrable barrier between him and the rest of the world, she thought with an instinct which seemed to come from nowhere.

'He sounds perfect.'

'I'm sure he is,' said Kate lightly. 'For someone who doesn't mind a man who looks arrogantly down his beautifully patrician nose at you!'

'Hmm! So you've got it bad!'

'Not really. A passing fancy,' answered Kate tightly. 'And anyway—I'll never see him again. Why should I?'

Never. It sounded so brutally final. Oh, what *magic* had he woven during that tense, short meeting? she wondered despairingly.

She had gathered up all her belongings and left the house in an unseemly rush, driven by some self-protective instinct which was quite alien to her. She had just known that if she didn't get out of the St John mansion quickly she risked making a very great fool of herself.

Because for one brief, mad moment as he and his godmother had accompanied her into the hall she had actually thought about *asking him out*!

Oh, not in the kind of 'would you like to go out with me?' way which was perfectly acceptable nowadays. Some of her more liberated girlfriends wouldn't have hesitated.

No, Kate would have been more subtle than that.

She could have said that she would be interested to see the latest Calverri silver catalogue on behalf of one of her clients. And that wouldn't have been a lie—she could think of at least half a dozen people who would doubtless love to choose something lavish and expensive from the latest glossy Calverri brochure.

But she had recognised in him a steely intelligence—and an innate ability to see what might lie behind a request such as that. He wasn't stupid. Women must react to him like that all the time—hence the contempt for her, which he had barely bothered trying to conceal.

So she had shaken his hand and given him a cool smile, and hoped that her body language hadn't betrayed the shimmering thrill of pleasure she felt to have his fingers closing around her hand.

She frowned as Lucy went to make some coffee, walking over to the window where the Thames glittered by in tantalisingly close proximity.

Flats like this didn't come cheap. Her own had been bought with the proceeds of her work after her salary had started surpassing even her wildest dreams. And everyone knew that you should put money into property.

She had the perfect job. The perfect home. And the perfect life.

So stay *away* from him, she told herself fiercely, and then she remembered that their paths were never going to cross again.

Thank God. Because she wasn't sure just how strong her will to resist him would be if they were to meet again.

Crazy.

Crazy to think that a man could arouse that amount of passion in a woman who was normally so self-controlled.

She turned to smile as Lucy carried in the tray of coffee and put him out of her mind with an effort.

Giovanni's mouth tightened imperceptibly as he put his foot down hard on the accelerator, and behind the smooth, dark curve of his sunglasses, the blue eyes glittered with irritation.

Damn!

And damn Kate Connors! Damn all women with eyes which invited so blatantly, and bodies just made to commit sin with.

He shook his head in denial, as if that could dispel the unmistakable ache of desire that had kept him teetering close to the hot edge of excitement since he had first seen the blaze of her fiery hair.

*He wanted nothing more to do with her!* And yet, even now he was speeding towards her flat. So why in the name of God was he carrying out his reluctant mission?

Because his godmother had asked him to, that was why. And all because the witch had left her Filofax behind. Again his mouth tightened. It was a laughably obvious ploy! She might as well have dropped her handkerchief to the ground in front of him. Or her panties, he found himself thinking and was cruelly rewarded with the hot, sharp stab of desire.

She must have known that his godmother would insist on his returning it, even though he had shaken his head unequivocally when she had first asked him.

'I cannot, Elisabeth,' he had told her.

'But, Giovanni, the poor girl will be lost without it! It's the size of an encyclopaedia!'

'Then why not post it to her?' he had suggested evenly.

'Because she'll need it,' said Lady St John with all the stubbornness of a woman who had spent her whole life getting her own way. 'And you virtually have to drive past her flat on your way back to the hotel, don't you? What time is your flight tonight?'

'At eight,' he admitted, resigning himself to the fact that he respected his godmother's wishes enough to back down on this. Though if any of his business colleagues had been there, they would have been very surprised to see him without his usual ruthless streak of determination.

'Well, then—you've got *hours*!' said his godmother brightly. '*Please*, Giovanni?'

'*Sí, sí, Elisabeth*,' he sighed, and held his immaculately manicured hand out with a rare smile. 'I will return it to her.'

He should have dropped the damned thing off on the way back to his hotel, but he didn't. Maybe if he had done that...

But instead he took a long, cool shower and changed from his suit into casual trousers and a fine shirt of purest silk that whispered like a woman's fingertips over his skin. And he shaved, and touched a musky-lemon scent to the pure, clean line of his jaw, though not for one moment did he ask himself why.

Nor why he went down to the bar and ordered a single malt whisky, then sat gazing at it, untouched, as though it contained poison.

He left for her flat just before six. That would just give him time to drop the Filofax off and then to drive straight to the airport. No time to linger. No time for coffee or the inevitable offer of a drink. Just a wry smile as he handed the Filofax over, a smile which told her that he knew exactly what her game was. And that he was far too experienced to fall for it.

But his pulse was hammering like a piston as he approached the turn off for her flat.

Kate left Lucy's flat and went upstairs to her own, where for once the glorious colour scheme failed to soothe her jangled senses.

She felt restless as she removed her cotton jacket. Itchy. Like a cat on a hot tin roof. As if there was a gaping hole somewhere deep inside her.

She changed from her hot and itchy clothes into one of her favourite outfits—a tiny green skirt and cashmere vest. It flattered her figure enormously, and as she stared into the mirror she found herself wondering what Giovanni Calverri would think of *that*!

No! This is just becoming *madness*, she told herself when she was back in the sitting room. With a shaking hand she poured herself a glass of wine and she had gulped down half of it before staring at the glass in a stupefied way that was completely alien to her.

She *never* drank on her own! Never!

She put the glass back down, with a hand that was no steadier, and walked through the sitting room into the small study which led directly off it, and sat down at her brand-new computer.

She logged on to the Internet and began tentatively pressing keys, until she reached the site she didn't even realise she was looking for, and one word flashed up on the screen in front of her, mocking her with memories of his lean, beautiful body.

Sicily.

On the screen in front of her, the island unfolded before

her eyes with the aid of the electronic equipment she now took for granted, and she printed out all the information available on the harsh beauty of a land which was known as 'Persephone's Island'. And then, with an odd thundering in her heart, and a prickling sense of expectation, she settled down and began to read.

Soon she was lost in tales of a bloody past, discovering the complex and stormy history of the sensual European island which lay so close to North Africa. Sicilians were the heirs of the ancient Greeks, Carthaginians, Arabs and Normans, she read. No wonder that Giovanni looked more spectacularly different from any other man she had ever met.

She was only disturbed by the insistent ringing of the doorbell and she blinked, and put the sheets of paper down.

Lucy, probably. She wasn't expecting anyone else—and in London no one ever seemed to call on anyone else unexpectedly. In fact, she had planned a quiet night as she always did at the end of a job. The celebration of its successful completion would come at the weekend, when they could lie in until late the next morning. They would go to their local bistro and eat chicken and drink a carafe of French country wine.

The doorbell rang again.

OK, she thought, I'm on my way! And if she hadn't been sure it was her sister she might have felt mildly irritated as she unplugged the Internet connection, but left the picture of Sicily still on the screen.

The ear-splitting sound had just invaded her ears for the third time, and her frown changed to one of worry. What was all the urgency?

With a wrench she pulled the door open, and her heart very nearly stopped.

It was him. Giovanni Calverri.

There.

On her doorstep, with the blue blaze from his eyes nearly

blinding her. Briefly she wondered whether those unbelievable, unusual eyes were a throwback to when the island had
been invaded by the Greeks, centuries ago, but she had no
time to wonder more, merely note the look of derision which
was hardening the luscious mouth.

'Y-you,' she breathed in a stunned kind of disbelief.

'But of course it is,' he concurred sardonically. 'Weren't
you waiting for me?'

'Waiting for you?' She prayed for logic and some kind of
strength to seep into her addled brain, but all she could think
about was his beauty. A hard, cold kind of beauty unlike
anything she had ever seen in her life. 'Why should I be
waiting for you?'

So she wanted to play games.

And, suddenly, so did he, damn her!

'Didn't you forget something?' he purred.

Right at that moment, she would be hard-pressed to remember her name. She felt a shivering awareness of him as
she shook her head distractedly. The lemony, musky scent
of him had invaded her nostrils like some kind of raw pher-
omone and she could sense the warm, male heat radiating off
him.

'I don't know what you're talking about.' She frowned.

Part of him wanted to ram the accusation home. To tell
her that he had no need of women who lacked such subtlety.
Predatory women with hungry green eyes. But that part of
him seemed to be fast on the wane and some alien emotion
was in the ascendancy.

Until he reminded himself that emotion had no place in
what was happening between them. He didn't know her. Or
particularly like her. Certainly didn't respect her. He just
wanted her, it was as simple and as complicated as that.

His lips parted to say with soft venom, Oh, yes, you do,
but some interloper had stolen the words from his mouth. He
raised his dark eyebrows questioningly and the hand which

had been partially concealed by the hard shaft of his thigh
suddenly withdrew and he held out the overstuffed black
leather diary towards her. 'This is yours, I believe?'

'My Filofax!' Kate stared at it in astonishment. Why, she
depended on it as she would her lifeblood—and she had been
in such a state that she hadn't even noticed it missing! 'I
didn't even realise I'd left it behind!'

She was a good actress, he would say that for her! For a
moment her surprise looked almost genuine. But her reaction
to him told him the true story. Should he taunt her with it?
Let her know that he could see through her schoolgirl games?
'You mean you hadn't missed it?' he mocked.

Kate stiffened, and indignation took the place of surprise.
'You think I left it behind on purpose?' she asked, her voice
rising with incredulity.

He shrugged, and the blue eyes glittered a challenge at her.
'Didn't you?'

She raised her eyebrows, scarcely believing what she was
hearing. 'Presumably just so that you would return it, I suppose?'

'If that was your intention.' He gave a coolly beautiful
smile. 'Then you have succeeded, mmm, *cara*?'

She almost laughed aloud at his arrogance. 'Maybe such
a scenario happens to you all the time *Mr* Calverri—'

'Giovanni,' he corrected softly, unable to stop himself
even though the distant clamour of his conscience told him
not to enter into this delicious game of flirtation.

'Maybe women *do* throw themselves at you—'

'They do,' he agreed gravely, and was rewarded with a
renewed look of outrage, though was unprepared for the
stealthy acceleration of his pulse as her sinful lips pursed
themselves together.

'Well, for your information—' she drew a deep breath,
slightly aware of behaving a little hypocritically since she
*had* been sitting here obsessing about him, hadn't she? '—if

I was *that* interested in a man I wouldn't resort to such transparent tactics, I would…would…'

Dark brows were raised in query as her words tailed off. 'You would…?'

Well, why not tell him the truth? 'I would have asked you out,' she said in a matter-of-fact voice.

Giovanni knew a moment of intrigue. Women *had* asked him out before, particularly English and American women, and he had always felt a sizzling disdain for such forward behaviour. Though a modern man in terms of accomplishments, he remained a staunch traditionalist at heart. The island of his birth defined the roles of the sexes far less markedly than in centuries past. But at its root still lay a machismo society where the man pursued the woman, and not the other way round.

And yet he found himself wondering if the unquestionably strong desire she had aroused in him might have enticed him enough to accept.

'But you didn't,' he stated softly.

Her eyes met his fearlessly. 'No, I didn't.'

But she had thought about it, he realised with a start. Mulled over the possibility and decided against it. He felt his interest flicker again, for wasn't that a kind of rejection?

His eyes narrowed. It was an entirely new sensation for him. No woman had ever rejected him, in any way, shape or form, and Giovanni felt the renewed leap to his senses as the first dull flush of the inevitable made him shrug in wry recognition.

'I will try not to be too offended at such a blow to my ego,' he murmured.

'Oh, thank heavens for that!' came her sardonic retort. 'I wouldn't have been able to sleep nights if you had!'

He almost smiled, acknowledging that something unknown and forbidden and dangerous was pulsing in the air around them. And that, instead of getting out of here as quickly as possible, he lanced through her emerald gaze with a cool look of challenge. 'So, aren't you going to ask me inside, *cara*?' And then realised just how shockingly and beautifully potent that question sounded.

'Inside?' she repeated slowly, and her mind started to play outrageous tricks on her as she imagined the reality of that simple, one-word request which suddenly sounded like the most erotic proposition imaginable. And didn't *cara* mean…darling?

He heard her momentary hesitation, knew what had prompted it and felt himself grow hard—so hard that he felt he might die with wanting her. But he pinned a lazy smile onto his mouth instead. A smile he didn't really mean, because the only thing that had any meaning at that precise moment was the need to possess her. A need he knew he should ruthlessly resist, and yet…yet…

'For a drink?' He shrugged, as though he could take it or leave it. 'As a reward for having come out of my way to see you.'

Some of the tension left her. Some but not all. She forced herself to open the door to him.

*Forced!* Just who did she think she was kidding? Why, if she gave into her true feelings right then she would have dragged him in by taking a great swathe of that silk shirt in her fist and drawing him close to her. So close that he would not be able to resist her.

But he *had* done her a favour. And wasn't she in danger of letting this all get a little out of hand? She should invite him into her home and expose herself to a little more of his own distinctive air of arrogance—*that* was the way to get him right out of her system! 'A drink?' She flashed him a bright, polite smile. 'Of course. Sure. Come in.'

He walked into her flat and it was as stunning as he had anticipated. He had known that her home would be exquisite, and it was. More than exquisite, it was distinctive. Like her.

Strong, bold colours which somehow managed to blend instead of grating on the eye. A mix and match which pleased and excited the senses. Again, like her.

She had changed, he noted, not for the first time—and now wore an indecently short skirt which showed off her long legs. A little vest-top in cool green cashmere emphasised the firm swell of her breasts and the way her torso tapered down to a delicious, tiny waist.

He swallowed and his eyes travelled almost with relief to a small table, where a half-drunk glass of wine rested. His mouth curved, he felt glad of the opportunity to disapprove of her again.

Kate noticed the tiny elevation of the jet-dark brows, felt his disapproval as surely as if it were shimmering in waves of heat off him. He didn't say anything—but, there again, he didn't have to. It was written clearly all over the autocratic features.

Some small inkling of who she really was came seeping back and she tried to catch hold of it, fast. Not some simpering schoolgirl, but a woman. His *equal*. 'Is something wrong, Giovanni?' she asked sweetly.

He shrugged. 'You drink alone?'

For one quietly hysterical moment she felt like saying that yes, yes, she *did* drink alone. That a bottle of vodka would leave her untouched and unsatisfied. Because she could tell from the unmarred perfection of his face and body that here was a man to whom excess would be anathema. Except perhaps for excess in one thing…

What could she say? That she never drank alone, but that he had unnerved her so much that she felt that wine might bring some warmth and some life back into her cold and bewildered veins?

'Rarely,' she conceded with an answering shrug, not caring whether he believed her or not.

Every instinct in his body was clamouring at him to get

the hell out. Telling him that here lay danger, a hot and inexplicable danger far beyond any he had ever encountered.
Giovanni had never known a moment's fear in all his thirty-
four years, but in that instant his flesh shivered with trepi-
dation at something quite outside his experience.

And yet he was known for his worldliness—his refusal to
be cowed by anybody or anything. So what spell was this
witch casting on him? Which honeyed chains were denying
him an exit from this enchanted place of hers? His head was
ordering him to leave and leave now, even as his body
bluntly refused to listen to such requests.

Kate saw the fevered glittering in his blue eyes. Take control, she thought. Take control. She drew a deep breath.
'What would you like to drink, Giovanni?' His name felt
delicious on her lips—so wickedly bewitching that just to
say it flooded her with the unturnable tide of desire.

He had asked for a drink and now that it was offered knew
that he must refuse it. And yet, like some disbelieving
watcher of his own self, he heard himself murmuring that
yes, yes—he would like a glass of wine very much indeed.

And then he lowered himself onto one of the sofas, and
watched her while she poured, his eyes following her closely,
intensely aware of every movement she made, bewitched by
her as he was rarely bewitched by a woman. The little skirt
she wore skimmed her thighs as she bent over, drawing at-
tention to the heart-stopping length of her legs.

Knowing that he watched her, Kate willed her hands not
to tremble as she slopped red wine into a simple-stemmed
glass of crystal and handed it to him.

'Thank you,' he said gravely and his pupils grew as dark
and as wide as a jungle cat's as she stood in front of him as
though she didn't quite know what to do next. 'Aren't you
going to sit down and join me, Kate?' he murmured.

How could such a mundane request sound like the most
erotic invitation she had ever heard? She perched on the edge

of the chair opposite him, and wrapped her fingers around the crystal glass.

He noticed the prim way that she had glued her knees together, and a pulse beat deep in his throat. He ran the tip of his finger thoughtfully around the rim of his glass. 'So what shall we drink to?'

For one mad moment, she thought that she saw humour lurking in the depths of those ocean-blue eyes, but the image dissolved almost before it had appeared and a cold hunger had taken its place once more.

'Hmm, Kate?' he prompted silkily. 'A toast to what?'

'I don't know,' she said tonelessly, thinking that her name could sometimes sound like a hard, shotgun sound, but the way that he curved his lips around it made it sound as soft and as beguiling as a caress. 'What do you usually drink to in Sicily?'

He smiled, but it was a smile without heart and now, at least, totally without humour. 'Why, we drink to the same things that people drink to all the world over, *cara mia*. To health. And to happiness,' he murmured, and raised his glass to her in a mocking gesture.

Leaving Kate wondering why the toast sounded such an empty one.

# CHAPTER THREE

KATE drank her wine more quickly than she had intended, or was used to. Not enough to be drunk—but enough to make her feel very slightly reckless.

But why not? She was committing no crime, was she? This man, whilst unknown to her, came with the excellent pedigree of being Lady St John's godson. He was an attractive man who fascinated her. So why not just enjoy the drink for what it was worth?

What did she think was going to happen?

That was the trouble—she just *didn't know*!

'It's very good of you to come out of your way,' she said, thinking how stilted her words sounded.

Giovanni opened his mouth to tell her that he was on his way to the airport and that the detour had been a minor one, but some instinct made the words remain unsaid. 'No problem,' he said obliquely.

'Shall I...shall I put some music on?'

Dismissively he shook his dark head and sipped at his wine, allowing his bright blue gaze to sweep around the airy room to where the reflection of light bouncing off the river dappled in pale gold waves across one wall.

'This is a very beautiful place you have,' he observed.

'Thank you.'

'And in an extremely desirable area.'

'Thank you again!'

His eyes narrowed. 'You must have done extremely well,' he observed thoughtfully, 'to be able to afford to live somewhere like this at your age.'

She wondered if she was imagining the inference behind

his casual statement. That maybe some *man* had set her up here? 'My success has so far outstripped my wildest dreams,' she told him truthfully. 'Perhaps in the same way as your own business fortunes? I expect you must be expanding all the time?'

He shook his head impatiently. 'No, we are not!'

'No?' she queried in disbelief. 'When your company's name is synonymous with the world's finest silverware? I'm not an expert—'

'No, you're not,' he agreed coolly.

'—but aren't you missing out on an opportunity?' she persisted, refusing to be cowed by his rudeness.

He shrugged as he acknowledged the compliment, noting almost reluctantly the way that her hair rippled in a fiery waterfall down over her breasts.

'Our company's success is based on traditional methods,' he told her softly. 'Over-expansion would be unwise—or so my father always maintained. We have never been a mass-market company, instead we make a limited number of very beautiful products. It is a lengthy and highly specialised process, and one of which my family is justifiably proud.' He thought how passionate his voice sounded. How he rarely gave so much of himself away to a stranger. Danger.

His fervour drew her irresistibly in and she found herself leaning forward, clasping her hands on her knees. 'How very romantic!'

Her face was earnest and the green eyes were huge and shining in her heart-shaped face. She looked, he thought with a sudden lurch of his heart, as eager and as animated as a child at Christmas. 'It is a little,' he agreed, with a slow smile. 'Though sometimes I have a battle to rein in my ambitions.'

'Beware of ambition which overreaches itself, Giovanni,' she chided softly, without thinking.

'Shakespeare,' he observed. '*Macbeth*.'

'You know the play?' She couldn't keep the surprise from her voice, and then saw the dangerous answering glitter of his eyes. 'I'm sorry, I didn't mean—'

He gave a wry smile. 'Oh, yes, you did,' he contradicted silkily. 'You'd placed me in your stereotypical little box, hadn't you, Kate? The sophisticated veneer merely masking the Sicilian peasant who lies beneath? More familiar with the Mafiosi than with any kind of literature? Is that what you thought?'

Her lips opened to deny it, but the harsh way he had spoken *had* stripped away the urbane sophistication of this elegant man who sat opposite her.

And suddenly she saw someone quite unlike any other who had come into the safe confines of her London life. She saw centuries of pride and of striving encapsulated in that lean, hard body, and that proud and beautiful face.

She could not tear her eyes away from him, observing him with the intense preoccupation she usually gave to a house she was about to decorate.

The muscles which rippled beneath the silk shirt were not the pretty-precious muscles of a man who worked out with weights at the gym every morning. This was a man as men were meant to be. Tough and sometimes harsh, and totally uncompromising.

And she found herself wondering how a man like this would treat a woman.

He saw the dull flush of awareness which had spread rosy wings across her high, pale cheekbones and he rose from the sofa before the dull ache of temptation grew stronger. 'May I use the bathroom?'

'But of course!' Thank heavens she had cleaned the sink that very morning! 'It's along the corridor—the third door down.'

Once there, he spurted icy water onto his wrists, as if doing that could subdue his heated blood. The eyes that stared back at him from the mirror looked like a stranger's eyes with their hectic glitter transforming blue to black.

She is just a woman, he told himself. A very beautiful woman, but a woman all the same. And he had resisted many, many women over the years.

On his way back to the sitting room he passed what was obviously her study. He noted that she had left her computer on, and then he heard a loud buzzing, like the muted sound of a dentist's drill, and saw a wasp as it battered uselessly at the window-pane.

He imagined its sting piercing her pale, smooth flesh and moved towards the insect, his mouth thinning as he acknowledged an inappropriate sense of protectiveness towards her. He raised the flat of his hand to crush the insect, and then relented, flicking the handle so that the window opened, and in that moment the wasp flew free.

As he shut the window he looked down at the scattered papers littered over the desk, and when an instantly familiar word leapt out at him he frowned.

Sicily.

His olive fingers flicked over the sheets and a warmth stole over him as he gazed at the familiar shape of the island. So she *was* interested in him! Interested enough to bother to come straight back here and look up the land of his birth.

In that one moment he knew that he could have her. Recognised and rejected the tantalising idea before it had a chance to move from mind to body.

He went back into the sitting room.

'It's time I was leaving,' he said abruptly.

Her heart lurched with disappointment, and Kate sprang to her feet. He looked so very right here, in her home—with his proud, dark beauty silhouetted against the golden backdrop of the light-dappled wall. Suddenly, she wanted him to stay.

'No, don't go! Not yet!' She saw him raise his eyebrows,

as if such demonstrativeness was faintly distasteful, but her desire not to lose him overrode any sense of maintaining an air of dignity.

'Please,' she continued, some instinct spurring her on as she put her hand out to rest in conciliatory fashion on his arm, and she shivered, for the muscle beneath was as honed as she had imagined it would be. Brazenly, she let the hand stay right where it was, her fingers curling around the curved, hard contour in a gesture which was most definitely possessive.

Their eyes met in a moment which was pure electricity, and she read the question that glittered so provocatively from the sapphire depths.

'I certainly didn't mean to offend you just now when I seemed surprised by your knowledge of literature,' she told him softly. 'Or to stereotype you. I've been very ungracious and you have been very kind.'

Giovanni narrowed his eyes as her words were made incomprensible by her touch. But then wasn't touch the most irresistible of all the senses? He looked down at where her hand rested lightly on his arm—a gesture at once so innocent and yet so profoundly sensual. He felt the almost imperceptible sting where her nails touched him and the blood begin to roar in his ears, because it was what he had wanted since the first moment he had set eyes on her.

To touch her.

No, more.

Much more than that. He wanted the most fundamental communion of all.

He felt the pull of temptation as something primitive flared into life inside him, like a dark, compelling fever which had taken over his body. And it had overtaken her, too—of that he was certain. He could see from the blackened pools which almost obscured the emerald of her eyes that she wanted him.

Really wanted him. In the space of a heartbeat he made his decision.

She would have him!

Very slowly and very deliberately he lifted his hand, and cupped her face in his palm as if he had every right to do so, grazing an arrogant thumb over the lush outline of her lips which trembled into immediate and urgent response.

Kate's knees turned unfamiliarly to water, her stomach warm and melting as desire flooded hotly through her veins and her hand fell redundantly to her side.

'Giovanni!' She swallowed, trying to tell herself that all he was doing was *touching her lips*, for heaven's sake!

His gaze was full-on, the blue eyes blazing with careless question. If she said no, then he would stop immediately. 'What is it, *cara mia*?' he purred, his accent as pronounced as it was persuasive. The pad of his thumb traced slowly around the quivering Cupid's bow of her mouth. 'What is it that you want from me?'

She trembled violently, unable to pull away, wondering just who *was* this new and over-responsive Kate? Must he think her a brazen fool? A woman who reacted so compliantly to a man she had just met. But suddenly, she *didn't care*! She shook her head, her mouth as dry as dust, as she struggled for words which would make sense of her reaction.

'Tell me.'

'It's a little difficult to say anything,' came her muffled response, 'when you're touching my lips like that.'

'You want me to stop touching them? Is that it?'

Her eyes met his with a fierce, burning look.

'No,' he answered, his accent deepening to one of soft reflection as his gaze dropped downwards, and he watched the flowering of her nipples through the cashmere vest. 'That is the very last thing you want, isn't it, *cara*? So tell me what you *do* want?'

What? Admit that she felt she would die if he didn't replace his thumb with his mouth, and kiss her? She opened her mouth to speak, but no words came, only the sudden erotic entry of his thumb between her lips, and she imprisoned it there with a fierce little suck, just like a baby.

'Or are you afraid to tell me?' He swallowed as he felt the moist plumpness of her mouth encasing his thumb.

For reply she sucked again, hard. She saw his responding shudder, heard the sigh which was very nearly a groan as he muttered a harsh imprecation in what she presumed was Sicilian.

She lifted her eyes to his. Afraid? All she knew was that she had never wanted a man so much and so unequivocably. She always played the respectable game. The getting-to-know-you-and-then-we'll-see game. Except that most times the getting-to-know-you bit had been enough to kill any desire stone-dead. And she always played by the rules, too—rules which Giovanni Calverri seemed hell-bent on redefining.

'Such an independent woman,' he teased, but there was a dark undertone to his taunt. 'With her fantastically successful company. Everything she wants, except the one thing she really, really wants—'

'You,' she breathed, the words coming out as thick and sweet as honey before she could stop them, 'I want you.'

His triumph at her admission was fused with despair. He had expected resistance—an appalled, outraged resistance. Not eager compliance so thinly disguised.

In the moment before he claimed her mouth he knew how doomed sailors must have felt, lured to their fate by sirens who tempted as this woman now tempted him.

He forgot his flight, forgot all about his reasons for flying home to Sicily. He felt the burst of desire which would not, could not, now be denied, and with a small angry growl he pulled her into his arms and began to kiss her.

In the dark heat of longing, she opened her mouth to his,

feeling the tension in his hard body. One taste and she knew that she was lost—it was that complete and that immediate.

'Oh, my God,' she moaned as his tongue began to trace a moist circle inside her lips.

'Your prayers will not help you now, *cara*,' he mocked, still with that slight edge to his voice. But as he felt her body melt closely into his he responded with a raw hunger which drove the last lingering traces of guilt away.

It seemed forever since he had kissed a woman, and these were new lips. Erotic lips. Lush and scented with wine. He groaned and plundered deeply, his hands tightening around the small indentation of her waist, unable to resist the curve of her hips and the cup of her bottom. He pushed up her skirt until the flat of his hands were exploring the cool globes laid bare by the thin, lacy thong she wore, and he felt that he might explode. 'You dress to kill,' he shuddered.

And she felt like she was dying. With need. And with pleasure. She felt her arms snake instinctively around his neck as her hips melded into the rocky power of him, thinking that it was too long since she had been in a man's embrace like this. She pressed her breasts against him, and he groaned, turning her in his arms and pushing her up against the wall, one lean, muscular thigh prising its way authoritatively between hers, and she felt the pooling of desire as it slicked against her thong.

She pushed him away from her, but only so that her fingers could fly to the buttons of his fine silk shirt, clumsily freeing them from their confinement, and he replied by swiftly unclasping and unzipping her skirt. It fell to her ankles immediately, and she stepped over it, wearing nothing now but a cashmere vest and a lacy thong.

With another small, angry growl of desire, Giovanni feasted his eyes on the front of the white thong, where the faint red triangle of hair tempted him from behind the flimsy lace. Her fingers were now scrabbling at his belt, and they were turning and touching like a pair of demented dancers, clothes falling free as they frantically kissed their way out of the sitting room.

He felt his hardness grow explosive, aware that their frenzied path had brought them to a door which he assumed must be to her bedroom.

Unprepared and unwilling to accept a moment's more delay, he scooped her up into his arms.

'Giovanni—' she gasped.

The blue-black eyes glittered obdurately. 'What?'

'Where are you taking me?' As she spoke the words, she knew that it was a foolish and redundant sentence, and his abstract, almost cynical smile told her that he felt exactly the same way.

'To bed,' he ground out, and kicked the door open.

# CHAPTER FOUR

GIOVANNI carried Kate straight over to the bed and put her into the centre of it, and, his eyes still holding hers with their icy glitter, began to unzip his trousers.

'You are protected?' he asked, as matter of factly as if he were asking her for a cup of coffee.

She shook her head. 'No.' Pointless to tell him that she had been single for over two years. He did not want a history of her love-life, he just wanted a practical answer to his question.

His eyes narrowed and he nodded almost thoughtfully as he withdrew a packet of condoms from his pocket, and Kate found herself wondering slightly wildly whether he was always so well prepared.

She lay there watching him. She knew that she ought to feel some sense of shame at what was happening. What she was allowing to happen to them, but her only sensation was one of glorious expectation. Even when his mouth twisted in another faint, cynical smile as he eased the zip carefully over his erection.

Wearing nothing but a pair of dark blue silken boxer shorts, he arrogantly kicked the trousers away from him and Kate heard herself gasping with unashamed pleasure as the boxers followed.

Greedily she ran her eyes over his naked body, focusing on the gleaming olive skin and a tight, taut torso. His shoulders were broad and his hips sensuously narrow, whilst the long, hard thighs were unbelievably lean and muscular.

He saw her watching him, and he deliberately touched himself. Saw the way that her eyes dilated as he stroked his finger arrogantly along his aching hardness, provocatively sliding on the sheath and turning practicality into eroticism. And then she lifted one pale, smooth thigh in unconscious invitation, and he could play that particular game no longer. 'You are wearing far too much, *cara*,' he told her softly as he climbed onto the bed next to her.

On an instinct she bent her head forward and licked luxuriously at the Adam's apple that curved at his throat, and felt him shudder beneath her tongue. 'Am I?' she whispered, transfixed by the hungry gleam in his eyes as he glittered a hungry gaze over her body.

'Much, much too much,' he murmured, his accent deepening. He peeled the cashmere vest over her head and felt the pounding of his heart as he caught his first sight of her breasts. So full and so pale. Encased in virginal white lace. His mouth twisted at the irony of that, but his thoughts were banished by the need of his body.

'*Matri di Diu!*' he muttered thickly, and dipped his head to her breast, unable to stop the quick flick of his tongue against the nub which strained so frantically through the delicate white lace.

'Oh!' The pleasure of his touch was so intense that it was almost like pain. No, not pain—because if this was pain, then how to define pleasure, pure and sweet? Her head fell back helplessly against the pillow as he flicked his tongue again.

'You like that, don't you, *cara*?' he enquired almost idly, watching the way that her hips moved against the bed in a frantic little circle, and the heat of his own longing almost made him lose his mind. 'Don't you?' he repeated harshly.

'Yes!'

He unclipped the bra and her breasts fell free, and once more he bent his head, taking the whole nipple greedily between his lips, and sucking on it hard, in an erotic imitation of the way she had sucked his thumb earlier, and Kate very nearly passed out with pleasure.

'Giovanni…' Her head moved from side to side on the pillow, as if in denial. No, not denial. She could deny this man nothing. Not a thing.

'*Sí?*' he whispered softly, but words failed her because he had moved his hand between her thighs and parted them.

She licked her lips feverishly as he moved his middle finger inside her thong.

And Giovanni's breath escaped him on a long, almost helpless shudder as he felt the syrupy desire of her slicking against his skin, feeling her shudder beneath his touch, hearing her moan his name once more. Was she like this for every man? he wondered for one hot and fevered moment.

He moved his finger experimentally against her. And again. And again. Her moans increased, and the sound of her helpless little cries made him grow even harder, almost unbearably so.

'I want you,' she whispered.

He gave an almost cruel smile as he lifted his dark head to look down at her. He would make her beg. Women liked to beg. 'Not yet,' he told her, on a silky taunt.

'Please.'

He shook his head. 'Not yet,' he repeated, on a low, provocative growl.

He wasn't going to stop what he was doing, Kate realised…

He wasn't going to stop…

And, to her utter disbelief, Kate felt the inexorable onslaught of fulfilment. The great tearing warmth of…of…

'Giovanni!' She said his name urgently. 'Oh!' She opened her eyes very wide. 'This is the best!' she gasped in astonishment. 'I'm coming…'

He could see that for himself from the sudden stiffening of her limbs, the way her back arched, the increased slick against his fingers, and then the slow, shuddering spasms which made her cry out loud.

He waited until she was nearly done, and then he straddled her, two taut thighs on either side of her hips, and thrust into her while her body was still pulsing with pleasure.

Her eyes flew open at the renewed sensation. He was so very big. So huge that he filled her completely. But, more than that, it felt so right to have him inside her. As though all her life her body had been yearning to have Giovanni Calverri make love to her like this.

He moved. Over and over. And as he moved he kissed her, and she gave herself up to the sweetness of those kisses, not thinking, not even caring about whether this was right or wrong, because nothing had ever felt this good.

He wanted to prolong it, to make it last forever. He had always been able to do that. Even as a teenager, when the newness of physical pleasure had threatened to overwhelm him. But now he felt the stealthy steal of orgasm come to claim him before he was prepared for it. He tried to fight it. For a moment he almost managed it. But when he felt her begin to pulse around him once more he knew that he was lost.

'Kate,' he said almost brokenly, the first and only time he had said her name since their bodies had joined with such bitter-sweet communion.

And Kate wept with some strange, deep emotion against his bare shoulder as she came again, feeling him begin to shudder deep inside her, arms closing around him tightly as she wished that this night could never end.

Giovanni awoke to unfamiliar shadows, his senses leaping into perception in a split-second as he tried to work out just where he was.

Dear God!

There was a sleeping woman beside him, which in itself was not strange, but he knew immediately that this was different. Her scent was different. The long red hair which the night had made dark was different.

And the sex had been different, too. Beautifully and irrevocably different.

Ruthlessly he quashed the memory as his body betrayed him once more with the stirring of desire, and he slipped silently from the bed.

He was of a race that understood secrecy. And stealth—and he had no difficulty moving without sound around the silent room to locate his clothes and shoes, which he carried from the room.

In the bathroom he dressed, glancing only once in the mirror, but once was enough. The wild glitter in his eyes told its own story. As did the darkened contours of his mouth, where she had kissed him as if she were drowning, as if she couldn't get enough of him.

His mouth twisted with self-contempt as he let himself noiselessly out of the flat into the crispness of the moonless summer night, and to where the black car was sitting reproachfully just as he had left it.

He looked up at the unlit windows of the flat as he turned the key and the engine flooded into powerful life, wondering whether she would appear, clutching a sheet perhaps, bewitching him with that pale and glorious body as she watched him drive away.

But the window remained empty, and relief coursed hotly through his veins, just as desire had heated them only hours earlier.

Two o'clock.

His flight to Sicily had long since departed. And there would be nothing now until the early morning. Night flights were banned—their intrusion into the quiet, sleeping skies around Heathrow not allowed.

He thought about what options lay open to him.

He could go to the airport and wait. Drink some unspeakable coffee while he contemplated his impetuous folly, and thought through the inevitable conclusion of what he had done.

But he shook his dark, gleaming head as if in answer to his unspoken question.

Inactivity would lie too heavily on his conscience.

And on his heart.

He accelerated as if he was aiming for some invisible finishing barrier and headed west.

He drove like a man on a mission—though he was cautious enough to observe the speed limit, but only just, even though the roads were empty of police cars. He had played the devil with fate once already tonight, and a speeding ban would end this remarkable night on an even more bitter note.

His body was still pulsing with the remembered warmth of her body and he uttered a soft curse in Sicilian as he felt the renewed ache of desire. But he forced it away, because the time for passion was now at an end, and he must address the consequences of his actions.

He had betrayed Anna with a woman he scarcely knew— so what did that say about him? More importantly, what did it say about their relationship?

He gave a sigh of regret mingled with anger. He had thought that his life with Anna had been happy—hell, it *had* been happy, but now for the first time he was compelled to acknowledge that something was missing from their life together, something which had never occurred to him was lacking until he had found it with someone else.

Passion.

The question was whether he was prepared to forgo passion and to cherish instead everything he had shared with Anna.

Or whether Anna deserved better.

He continued to drive though he did not know where, only that the miles eaten up by the machine did nothing to ease his sense of wrongdoing. And it was only when daylight began to break in purest gold shot with rose-pink over the horizon that he slowed down and began to follow the signs back towards the airport.

Unfamiliar light woke her. The cold, clear light of dawn as it flooded through the uncurtained windows.

Kate blinked, her body warm and aching, her mind drifting in and out of sweet, remembered places, and then her eyes flew wide open to greet the pale and brilliant light of early morning as memory slipped sharply into focus, at the same time as did one monumental and heartbreaking fact.

He had gone! Giovanni had gone!

Her heart clenched painfully in her chest and she closed her eyes. Please, please, please…let him still be here, she beseeched in silent prayer.

She held her breath, but the flat remained utterly silent save for the almost imperceptible ticking of the bedside clock whose illuminated face showed that it was almost five in the morning.

She shivered as she remembered what she had done. What *they* had done. Without thought. And without shame, she told herself fiercely. Maybe it had not been textbook relationship behaviour as taught to her by her mother, but she could not— and would not—regret it.

She pushed the rumpled sheet back and found herself staring with helpless longing at the indentation of where his head had lain on the pillow. She ran the flat of her hand over it, as if that faint touch could magic him back again. And she found herself understanding why women sometimes kissed the pillow on which their lover had rested his head.

She shuddered a breath as hope flared foolishly in her heart. Maybe he *was* in the bathroom.

But a closer glance around the room killed that hope stone-dead. Only *her* discarded clothes lay scattered wantonly all over the carpet of the bedroom.

Her cheeks flushed.

It had been beautiful. Passionate and profound. She had felt proud to love him, and had imagined that the feeling had been mutual. A man and a woman sent spinning out of orbit by the power of their mutual attraction.

But if that was the case, where was he now?

She licked at her dry lips distractedly. He had been on his way back to Sicily, she reasoned. Perhaps his business had been of a particularly urgent nature, and he had not wanted to disturb her. Because some unshakable instinct told her that Giovanni Calverri was far too fastidious a man to ever indulge in the transient pleasures of a one-night stand. Why, she had certainly never done anything like it herself!

Which meant that he would almost certainly have left a note.

Her heart was beating very fast as she went from room to room, switching on every light as she did so, so that no surface would go unsearched.

Until she was forced to admit to herself the ghastly, horrible truth.

That Giovanni had left without a trace.

And that was when pain began to metamorphosise into anger...

Giovanni lifted his eyes to the dark-haired stewardess, and frowned, barely noticing the overt look of admiration she was slanting at him. 'What?' Automatically, he had lapsed into Sicilian.

Her eyes flashed excitedly as she heard the distinctive dialect, but she was only able to answer him in Italian. 'I asked whether you would like a cup of coffee before take-off?' she said in a smooth, practised voice.

What he wanted was for the damned plane to be touching down on the soil of his homeland—and certainly not a flight which involved a changeover in Rome while he waited for a connection.

For half a moment he had considered chartering a private jet to take him on from Rome, but another sharp jab of his conscience had stopped him. Was he really about to start rewarding his outrageous indiscretion with a flamboyant gesture of extravagance?

'Please,' he said shortly.

She prettily offered him a tray of pastries but he waved them away with an impatient hand, and spent the rest of the flight forcing himself to go through a batch of papers which could easily have waited.

But he needed something to occupy his mind. Something to try to stop him remembering the red blur of her hair and the emerald gleam of bewitching eyes.

You're going home, he told himself. With all that that entails.

In Rome, he forced himself to eat a little something, reminding himself that he had had nothing since yesterday's lunch. But the food tasted bland, and he pushed the half-touched plate away as his flight was announced.

The minutes ticked by like hours as Kate prowled around the flat, her initial sense of desolation gradually being replaced by a feeling of outright fury.

How dared he?

How *dared* he?

By such a cold and uncaring rejection he had reduced a wonderful night to the bitter realisation that she had indulged in a classic one-night stand.

And then been dumped!

She felt her cheeks stain with shame. They were both mature and consenting adults. OK, he might have decided that he didn't want to see her again, but at least he could have done her the courtesy of going through the motions of civ-

ilised behaviour. It wouldn't have killed him to have breakfast with her, surely? Or to have made love to her when she
woke up? prompted the hungry voice of her senses. He could
have taken her telephone number and said that he would ring
her, even if he hadn't meant it.

Bastard!

She couldn't sleep, eat, or concentrate on anything. She
ran a bath and afterwards threw on a pair of jeans and a
T-shirt—and the more she thought about Giovanni's behaviour towards her, the more her fury grew and grew. But fury
seemed to hurt less than shame—and far less than the pang
of realising that she would probably never see him again.

She couldn't understand it. Had she misread everything?

He had been the best lover she had ever had, and she was
certain that the experience had been as wonderful for him as
it had been for her. She had seen that almost dazed sense of
wonder on his face as their bodies had joined together.

So why creep out like a thief into the night and destroy
what they had shared? Why leave her with the bitter taste of
rejection and confusion?

Several times that day she reached her hand out to the
telephone, then decided against using it when she reminded
herself that men like Giovanni Calverri had it much too easy.

How would he ever learn that he couldn't just go around
taking what he wanted without showing a little more consideration in the process? Unless somebody actually had the
nerve to tell him?

And the unthinkable notion that she might just be one in
a long line of broken-hearted international conquests was
enough to make up her mind.

Resolutely, Kate reached her hand towards the telephone
again, only this time she picked it up.

'International directories, please,' she said crisply.

*      *      *

Giovanni drew to a halt in front of the Calverri headquarters, and wondered why everything felt different.

Why *he* felt different.

Yet outwardly nothing had changed. Heat sizzled off the parched earth and the sky was a dazzling blue as he stared at the huge, old, cloistered villa set in a magnificent piece of land where his family's silver business was housed. Here, artisans who had been with the company for most of their working lives lovingly created silver heirlooms using traditional methods which had never been bettered.

And every spring students would flock from all over the world to learn their craft at the hands of experts. From these students would be drawn fresh blood and talent which would keep the Calverri business running long into the next century.

Giovanni sighed as he made his way to his secretary's office. His heart was heavy, and the burden of guilt weighed down on him like lead. Soon he was going to have to face Anna and he just didn't know what he was going to say to her.

His secretary looked up as he came in, and her eyes widened with pleasure.

'Giovanni, you're late!' she exclaimed, her smile of welcome dying on her lips as she saw the look on his face. 'What has happened?' she questioned. 'Is something wrong?'

Was it that apparent, then? What had happened to his ability to hide his feelings—to present a cool, remote kind of demeanour—so that people never knew what he was thinking?

'A long journey,' he said, and shrugged, picking up a handful of documents in a gesture designed to guard against further intrusion. 'What needs to be gone through? I had better catch up on whatever is urgent, and then I must go and see Anna.'

His secretary smiled. Once she had entertained romantic notions about Giovanni herself, but then reality had set in.

He was her boss—an untouchable god of a man. And she adored Anna. Everyone did.

'Did that order go off to Texas?' he quizzed.

'As scheduled.' She nodded.

'And what of the Scandinavian project?'

'Better than expected.' She smiled back.

His satisfied nod was more automatic than genuine, and he worked away with a quiet determination until all the backlog was cleared and he knew he could put off the moment of truth no longer. He rose to his feet.

'I will see you tomorrow, Gabriella.'

His secretary narrowed her eyes in silent question, but said nothing other than, '*Sí*, Giovanni.' And she sat watching as he left the office, disturbed only by the sudden intrusion of the telephone, which she picked up.

'*Pronto*!'

On the other end of the line, Kate felt her nerve nearly fail her, but some dogged determination drove her on. 'Do you...do you speak English?' she enquired falteringly.

'But of course!' There was a slight pause. 'Who do you wish to speak to?'

Kate drew a deep breath, and the name came out in a gush. 'Giovanni Calverri! Is he there, please?'

'Who is calling?'

Kate thought how frosty the voice had become. Should she leave her name? 'Is he there, please?' she asked again.

There was a loud, undisguised sigh, as if the person at the other end of the line had scant patience with unknown women who refused to say who they were.

'No, he is not here!'

'And are you expecting him back?'

'Not today.' There was a pause. 'Signor Calverri has been in England.'

I *know*! Kate bit the words back.

'And has only just arrived back.' Another pause. 'So obviously, the very first thing on his mind was to go and see his fiancée.'

His *fiancée*? 'Oh, I see,' said Kate faintly, as, with a slow, sinking pain in her heart, she put the receiver down without another word.

# CHAPTER FIVE

GIOVANNI watched the woman who walked alongside the pool towards him.

She was the epitome of elegance—her pure silk dress in a buttery-cream colour setting off the raven-dark hair and the huge, black-fringed brown eyes. Her face was serene, on her lips a smile of calm acceptance—an easy pleasure at seeing once more the man she had known for all her adult life.

He felt the deep, sharp pain of regret.

'Giovanni!'

'Hello, Anna.'

She moved straight into his arms, but he could not bring himself to hold her other than awkwardly, as if she were composed of some brittle substance, and his touch might contaminate her. She pulled away, her brow criss-crossing in a frown.

'What is it, *caro*?' she demanded.

What way to tell her? Though the notion of *not* telling her was even more unthinkable.

He knew that most men of his acquaintance would put the whole experience down to a fleeting temptation of the flesh, not worth confessing to because of the consequences of such a confession. But Anna was the woman he knew. The woman he had always intended to marry.

'Giovanni!' She was looking at him now in alarm. 'What has happened to make you look this way? Is someone sick? Has something happened to the business?'

He met her stare without flinching, and it was perhaps because she knew him so well, and had known him for so long, that a horrified look of comprehension began to dawn in her dark eyes.

Her voice grew faint. 'Tell me!'

He had no desire to hurt her, but hurt was an irrevocable repercussion of his actions. His mouth hardened. 'I met someone—'

He heard her pained intake of breath, and he flinched as he saw the hurt that clouded her eyes.

'And...' He hesitated, trying to pick out the least wounding words of all.

'And what? The truth, Giovanni!' she demanded, in as furious a tone as he had ever heard.

'*I slept with her!*'

There was a short, shocked silence before she spoke.

'How many times?'

Her question astonished him. 'What?'

'You heard me! How many times did you sleep with her?'

'Once,' he answered heavily. 'Just the once.'

'Only once?' She frowned at him in disbelief.

'*Once!*' he emphasised bitterly, his blood heating his veins with shameful pleasure.

She shook her head and let her eyelids flutter down to conceal her eyes. 'Oh, why did you have to tell me?' she whispered.

His heart beat strong with the burden of guilt. 'You needed to know the truth.'

But she shook her head once more. 'No, Giovanni,' she said acidly. 'You needed someone to share the burden with, didn't you? To ease your conscience! Most men would have filed it away under an experience never to be repeated—especially if, as you say, it was just the once.'

But her words leapt out at him like tiny barbs. *If, as you say...* She would never trust him again. He knew that. The rest of her life would be spent watching him. Waiting for him to slip. Always wondering...

'Anna, I'm sorry—'

'No!' she retorted furiously. 'You have offloaded your guilt—please spare me your need for forgiveness!' She sank down on one of the wrought-iron benches that stood in the shade of a cypress tree. Then looked up at him with hurt, bewildered eyes.

'Who is she?'

'No one!'

'*Yes! Somebody!*'

'A girl. Just a girl I met in England and—'

She cut across him icily, 'Was she the first?'

He stared at her incredulously and then his eyes narrowed dangerously. 'Of course she was the first!'

'There's no "of course!" about it!' She studied the engagement ring on her finger, then looked up at him, her gaze very steady. 'The first? And only?'

Giovanni could see the hurt in her eyes, but there was, he realised, no surprise whatsoever. Almost as if she had been *expecting* him to stray. His mouth hardened as he thought of all the women he had turned down over the years. One misdemeanour, and you were scarred by it forever. And he had only himself to blame.

And Kate, of course, he thought with a kick of something akin to both hatred and desire. Kate with those smooth, pink nails which had curled around his arm so possessively, enchaining him with the sweet seduction of her touch.

'The first,' he agreed quietly. 'And the only.'

'Oh, why did you have to tell me, Giovanni?' she whispered sadly and again he felt the sharp pang of remorse as she saw the white glitter of the diamond which sparkled on her finger. 'Most men would have tried to get away with it.'

'Because I could not bear to live a lie with you, Anna,' he told her softly, and a muscle worked in his cheek as he silently cursed the day his path had crossed with that of Kate Connors.

*     *     *

Back in London, Kate sat staring at the telephone as if it were an alien just landed from Mars.

Engaged, she thought in a frozen kind of disbelief, starting as the doorbell began to ring, and she remembered the last time it had rung like that.

Like a zombie, she walked out to answer it, some stupid hope making her wish that history could repeat itself and that Giovanni would be standing there, telling her that there was no fiancée. That she had made a terrible mistake.

But it was Lucy, her copper hair pulled back into a ponytail, and not a scrap of make-up on her face—but that didn't matter, thought Kate. Not when your eyes were like emeralds sparkling in such a pale, clear face.

'Hello, Lucy,' she said, and then her voice began to tremble.

Lucy swept her a swift, assessing look and her face took on a mixture of concern and anger. 'You've seen him, haven't you?'

'Who?'

'Giovanni Calverri!' Lucy spat the name out.

'Seen him?' Kate very nearly laughed, but tears were much too close to the surface to allow her the luxury of laughter. 'Yes, you could say that I've seen him.'

Lucy came into the flat and shut the door behind her. 'And?'

Kate bit her lip. Who else could she tell? Who else could she bear to tell? Someone who loved her enough never to judge her. And Lucy did.

She tried to recount the whole sorry story matter-of-factly. 'He turned up yesterday after I'd been to see you.'

Lucy nodded. 'Go on.'

'He... I... We...' Kate shook her head and tried again. There was no pretty way to phrase it. 'We went to bed,' she said simply.

'You *what*?' breathed Lucy.

'You sound shocked,' commented Kate drily.

'That's because I am! Oh, no,' she amended suddenly as Kate's lips began to tremble again, 'not because of what you did—but because it's just not like you!'

'I know it isn't.'

'You're the kind of woman who plays safe, Kate. Gosh, I remember when you were going out with Pete—he used to say that you'd virtually interviewed him on at least the first four dates before you would even let him *kiss* you!'

Kate nodded. 'Yep. That's me. Safe, sensible Kate.'

Lucy knotted her fingers together. 'So what happened? What was so different?'

'He was,' said Kate quietly. She walked over to the window and stared unseeingly at the river before she turned round to face the soft consternation in her sister's eyes and tried to explain the inexplicable. 'It was an attraction like no other I'd ever felt. Ever.'

'And he must have felt the same way too, presumably?'

'That's what I thought,' agreed Kate tonelessly, and realised that she couldn't give Lucy only half the story. Didn't want to, either. And who would she be protecting if she kept the horrible, hurtful truth to herself? Only a man who didn't deserve one vestige of protection. 'But he disappeared in the middle of the night.'

Lucy's face fell. 'He did a runner?'

'He certainly did.'

Lucy thought for a moment, then she shrugged awkwardly. 'Maybe he had a good reason—'

'Oh, a very good reason!' Kate gave a hollow laugh. 'Like the fact that he's engaged to be married—that's reason enough!'

Lucy winced. 'You *are* joking?'

Their eyes met.

'I'm sorry, Kate, I didn't mean to be flippant. As if you'd

joke about something like that. But how do you know? I mean, you surely didn't—'

'You think I went to bed with him *knowing* that he was going to be married to someone else?'

Lucy shook her head. 'Of course I didn't!'

'*He should have told me,*' whispered Kate. 'He should have told me that he was promised to someone else!'

'How on earth did you find out?'

This was the humiliating part. Kate swallowed. 'I was angry—angry with him for having left without even so much as a goodbye, and angry with myself for having behaved so *outrageously*. I decided that he needed to be told he just couldn't do something like that—if not for my sake, then maybe he might just think about it with the next poor girl he bowls over with his charm!'

'So you rang him?'

Kate nodded. 'In Sicily. I got some snotty secretary who told me smugly that he had gone off to see his fiancée—'

'Maybe she was lying,' said Lucy hopefully.

Kate put her head to one side as she looked at her sister. 'Oh, sure! Why would she do a thing like that?'

'Because some secretaries are madly in love with their bosses themselves, and so they take it on themselves to be as beastly as possible to other women!'

'Nice try, Lucy, but I don't believe she was lying.' There had been other clues, too. She should have given them more thought. The way that the attraction he had undoubtedly felt towards her had held the unmistakable trace of antipathy. His reluctance to stay once he had dropped off her Filofax. His offensive arrogance in assuming that she had left it behind deliberately. Believing that she wanted to lure him. And her behaviour towards him had probably seemed as though she *had* wanted to lure him here.

What man would pass up on an offer like that?

'So what will you do?' Lucy's face crumpled. 'Oh, God—Kate, you couldn't be...*pregnant*, could you?'

Kate shook her head, because even *that* hurt to tell. 'Oh, no,' she said bitterly. 'No chance of that. Signor Calverri conveniently had a packet of condoms on him! No doubt always prepared for the unexpected!'

'It's a rather good thing, under the circumstances,' observed Lucy drily. 'The last thing you need in a situation like this is an unwanted pregnancy.'

Kate's mouth crumpled. 'I don't know what to do,' she admitted, thinking that for a man who was little more than a stranger the pain he had caused seemed to be disproportionately intense.

'Nothing you can do,' said Lucy in a determinedly bright voice. 'Except carry on working and waiting for Mr Right and put it all down to experience.'

'There's no such thing,' said Kate bitterly.

'What, as experience?'

She swallowed, trying to smile and to lighten up. Maybe tomorrow. Or the next day. But just now her sense of shame and humiliation was too strong for her to be able to resist cynicism. 'As Mr Right,' she said tightly. 'Now, are we going out tonight?'

'You want to?'

Kate shrugged. 'We always do at the end of a job, don't we? I can't sit around here moping for the rest of my life!'

Once Lucy had gone, she made a determined effort to dress up, even though her heart wasn't in it. She nearly wore black, but that seemed like a psychological admission of defeat. So she put on white linen trousers instead—with a glittery little top in silver-spangled white, because the summer night was warm and sultry.

At just past eight she and Lucy set off for the Italian restaurant, stopping off at the pub on the way as they always did.

It was a typical London pub—packed and noisy—so they sat outside on a wall next to a big pot of daisies and drank their lager and enjoyed the river view.

'I've never seen you look so fed-up, Kate,' said Lucy, watching her sister stare miserably into the foamy top of her drink.

'I guess I've been very lucky in the heartbreak stakes,' said Kate lightly. 'Up until now.' Her infrequent love affairs had tended to become friendships more than the mad kind of passionate romances which broke your heart. She had never been the type to sob into her pillow over a man.

So how come one brief and beautiful encounter had left her feeling as though a part of her had been torn out and thrown into the gutter? Her eyes glimmered with unshed tears, and she forced herself to take another sip of beer.

'Come on, Kate,' said Lucy gently. 'Let's go and eat.'

# CHAPTER SIX

AT LEAST Kate had her career. That was what she kept telling herself over and over again, in an attempt to convince herself that in work lay some kind of refuge from her problems. The only difficulty being that her particular career was that it was such a solitary occupation.

When she decorated a house she liaised with the owners to discover exactly what it was they wanted her to create. She then went about finding paints and fabrics and *objets d'art* from various suppliers.

But there was no regular daily interaction with workmates. No one to sit and drink coffee with and talk.

Though maybe that was a blessing in the circumstances. Workmates might ask her why her eyes were ringed with great black shadows. Why eating seemed to be an intolerable effort. And why it took all her energy just to summon up a fraction of her usual enthusiasm.

She was now refurbishing a dining room in north London—a sprawling great Edwardian house belonging to a television actor and his presenter wife. Money was no object, and they had seen some of her work at friends' houses and given her a free rein. The dream scenario, really. But this time the smile she pinned to her face each morning felt like an effort, and she hoped that her mood wasn't transmitting itself to her employers.

On Friday, when the walls had been painted in a rich, dark green, she returned to her flat in Chiswick and thought unenthusiastically about the weekend ahead. She needed to keep active. To fill her time, so that the memory of Giovanni and his bright blue eyes and delicious body would fade far away into the distance.

She thought about going to visit her parents. No. That was a crazy idea. Her mother would take one look at her gaunt face and demand to know exactly what was wrong—and how could you tell your mother something like *that*?

The phone began to ring and aimlessly she reached out her hand and picked up the receiver, trying to inject enthusiasm into her voice. 'Hello?'

There was a click as the line was disconnected and she stared at it for a moment, then replaced it uninterestedly, secretly pleased that no one had spoken. The last thing she had felt like doing was having a conversation, having to pretend that everything was all right, when everything in her heart felt all wrong.

The heat of the summer day was still intense, and so she drew herself a bath and soaked in it for ages, until the water was merely lukewarm and the tips of her fingers had shrivelled into pale little starfish. Then she put on a long satin robe and padded barefoot into the sitting room.

She would order in some pizza. She winced. No, definitely not pizza. The Italian connection would be much too great to contemplate. A curry, then. And a glass of wine. With maybe a sad old movie afterwards, which would allow her to shed tears legitimately.

She painted her toenails and had just let them dry, when the doorbell rang, and she hoped it might be Lucy. She didn't want to hassle her sister with her problems, and so she hadn't suggested getting together with her. But maybe Lucy fancied a little company as well.

But it wasn't Lucy who stood on the doorstep, it was Giovanni, and Kate stared at him, her mouth drying, her heart beginning to thunder as she met a hard blue gaze.

'You!' she breathed.

'Me,' he agreed sardonically.

Her mouth had difficulty forming the words. 'Wh-what are you doing here?'

His mouth thinned. What did she think he was doing here? His gaze moved slowly from her face to her body, and the lush swell of her breasts straining against silver-grey satin drove the dull ache of suppressed desire into a heated beat against his temple. He chose his words carefully. 'I had business to see to in England.' His eyes mocked her. 'And I thought I might drop by, as I was passing.'

She knew exactly what he was implying. Oh, the arrogance! The unmistakable predatory assumption of the man! Kate leaned on the door and composed her face into a calm, unperturbed mask made false by the sustained thundering of her heart. 'So here you are,' she observed coolly.

Her haughty demeanour stirred his senses more than it had any right to. Had he expected that she would simply fall into his arms? 'Here I am,' he agreed levelly. He paused deliberately, and his voice deepened into a silky question. 'Are you not going to invite me in, *cara*?'

She supposed that some women might have shouted a few home truths before slamming the door in his face, but her curiosity was aroused. *And not just your curiosity,* taunted the remorseless voice of her conscience with chilling accuracy. Despairing of the fact that the last thing she wanted was for him to simply walk away, she shrugged nonchalantly.

'Why not?' She opened the door wider, telling herself that it was necessary to see him. To talk to him. What did they call the kind of conversation they needed to have together? Closure, that was it. Common sense told her that she would never completely be free of his memory unless they achieved some kind of closure. That was all it was. She gestured for him to come inside.

Silently he expelled the breath which he hadn't even realised he had been holding, and followed her into the sitting room, his eyes mesmerised by the swaying thrust of each buttock as it moved provocatively against the satin while she walked.

Her heart was beating fast. His presence was like a light, filling the room with some unbearable, shimmering promise. And that was an illusion, she told herself fiercely as she turned to face him, wondering whether her face betrayed the fact that she wanted him.

He was wearing some unspeakably elegant suit in a soft dove-grey. And a thin white shirt through which she could just discern the faint shadowing of the hair which she had scraped her fingernails against at the moment of orgasm. A tie of sapphire almost as blue as his eyes had been loosened, and it exposed a gleaming little triangle of olive flesh. There was nowhere to look but at him, and she forced herself to swallow down desire, and to remind herself instead of the true situation.

But the words still hurt to say. 'So what about your fiancée, Giovanni?' she enquired deliberately. 'Does she know you're here? With me?'

The memory of Anna, and the hurt he had caused her, filled Giovanni with heated regret. But something else heated him too—the same accursed reason which had brought him to her bed in the first place.

'Ex-fiancée,' he corrected icily.

'Oh, dear—I'm so sorry! Still, I guess it's better she found out about you sooner rather than later.'

He stilled, then raised dark brows, and the insult freed him, made what he was about to do seem ridiculously simple. 'Found out about me?' he echoed silkily. 'And just what is that supposed to mean, *cara*?'

He made the word *cara* sound like a profanity. 'What do you think it means?' she demanded, remembering how he had whispered that word to her over and over. 'I'm not flattering myself to think that I was the first little dalliance you'd had on the side!'

Tension tightened his tall, dark frame. His voice was velvet, edged with steel. 'You think that I am the kind of man to regularly commit infidelity, do you, Kate?'

'How should I know? I hardly know a thing about you!' But as soon as the words were out of her mouth she realised that she had dug her own grave of shame.

'No, you don't,' he agreed, and his eyes gave an insolent glitter. 'But that didn't stop you being as intimate with me as it is possible for any woman to be!'

Kate flinched as if he had struck her. But how right he was. She recalled the way she had touched him. Licked him. Sucked him in a place where she had sucked no other man. She felt the colour rush to her cheeks as pride made her construct her own defence against the accusation.

'Do you really think I would have…would have…' she struggled to find the least offensive way to describe what had happened '…would have slept with you if I'd known that you were engaged to be married?'

Her question brought the night back into sharp focus with exquisitely arousing clarity. 'We had very little sleep that night, as I remember, *bella*—you were delightfully eager to repeat the experience over and over again.'

'So were you!'

'Who would refuse such an offer when it was so enticingly offered?' He shrugged. 'But how could I possibly make a judgement about your morality? This bizarre situation is entirely mutual—and, as you just so sweetly pointed out, we barely know each other. At least, not in the conventional sense.'

But the assumption was crystal-clear. Kate flicked angry fingers through the red fall of her hair, only succeeding in making it even more dishevelled than it already was. 'You think I'm some sort of tramp who gives her body to any man who comes along?'

'Not any man,' he corrected, with a shake of his dark head.

'I recognised that you had exquisite taste, right from the beginning. I cannot condemn you for your choice of partner, Kate.'

It took a moment for his words to sink in. 'You're very arrogant.'

He shook his head. 'No. Just honest.'

'But not honest enough to tell me at the time that you were engaged?'

'I wasn't thinking very straight at the time.'

'No.' She stared at him, shocked by how much she wanted to touch him. Wondering just what she would do if he touched *her*. 'Just what *are* you doing here, Giovanni?'

He caught the blinding green question in her eyes, and a pulse began to hammer at his temple. 'I think you know the answer to that very well, *cara*,' he said softly.

There was silence, save for the deafening thunder of her heart. Yes, she knew. She had known ever since she had opened the door to him and seen the predatory glitter in his eyes. Just as she had known the last time, too.

And there didn't have to be a repeat performance.

She lifted her chin and said with surprising calm, 'You think I'm going to fall into bed with you again?'

He thought that bed had nothing to do with it. To do it right there where they stood would do fine to begin with. 'Why not?' He gave a slow, cold smile. 'You know you want to.'

His assessment quite literally took her breath away. But only for a moment. 'You rate yourself very highly as a lover, don't you, Giovanni?'

The smile was now edged with ice. 'You told me so yourself. In fact, you gave me the very highest recommendation— *you said that I was the best.*'

He spoke nothing more than the truth. She remembered her frantic little pleas, the sighed pleasure, and the indolent little murmurs of praise she had whispered into his ear just after she had…had…

'I didn't know then that you were engaged—'

'Would you have cared?'

'Of course I would have cared!'

He shook his head. 'I don't think so. You just wanted me,' he taunted. 'Very badly. As badly as I wanted you.' Still want you. 'You curled your fingers around my arm and I knew then that you would not have been satisfied until I had pleasured you as no other man had before.'

'That was just a touch!' she protested. 'An innocent touch! I hardly started removing my clothes in front of you, like some kind of temptress!'

The ache intensified. 'Don't be so naïve! It is never ''just'' a touch. And never, ever innocent! How could it have been, when the chemistry between us was so strong? You were fascinated by me. Intrigued by me.'

'You can't know that!' she said inadequately.

'Can't I?' He paused. 'I saw the print-out from your computer.'

She stared at him with a look of incomprehension. 'What print-out?' she said blankly.

'You'd been doing your homework on me, hadn't you, Kate?'

Still she didn't get it.

'And reading up about Sicily,' he told her in a soft, taunting voice. 'You clearly wanted to know something of my land and its people—presumably to learn a little more about me. You wanted as much background on me as you could and I cannot deny that I wasn't flattered.'

'I don't believe I'm hearing this!' she declared. 'You'd been positively *insulting* about the fact that I knew nothing about Sicily—and just because I wanted to fill in a few gaps in my knowledge you make it sound like I had some kind of master-plan to ensnare you!'

'You didn't need a master-plan, Kate,' he told her starkly. 'Your eyes ensnared me from the first moment I looked into them.'

She was very nearly beguiled by the velvet caress of his compliment, until she reminded herself that he had betrayed his fiancée, and in a way he had betrayed *her*, too. If, as he had acknowledged, the chemistry between them had been so strong, then why had he asked to come in for a drink in the first place? He must have recognised that he was placing himself in a dangerous situation.

And her.

Unconsciously she tightened the belt of her satin robe around her waist, but the flicker of his eyes as he followed the movement of her fingers told her that it was entirely the wrong thing to do. He was staring at her as if he would like to undo what she had just done, and to...to...

'I think you'd better leave now,' she told him huskily.

Leave? An earthquake would not have budged him. He shook his head and moved towards her, and she was frozen with wanting and longing.

'No,' she whispered. 'Giovanni, no.'

'Oh, yes,' came the silky contradiction. 'Yes, Kate.'

She shook her head, but it was too late, and he was pulling her into his arms and bending his head to hers and she supposed that she could have stopped him. Should have stopped him. But no power in the world could have prevented her lips from parting in a sharp little gasp of remembered pleasure as he drove his mouth down like a man who had been starved of kisses.

She swayed within the circle of hands which impatiently drew her in towards the hard cradle of his desire, and felt the immediate flowering of need as his tongue licked its way inside her mouth.

He tried to tell himself that kissing her was the only way to ensure her capitulation, but that was only a part of it because he could not seem to stop himself. Was dazed by it. A kiss that had started out hard and hungry became luxuriant and soft—the erotic brushing together of two tongues intent on some slow, sensual exploration. And it sparked off an inevitable chain of reaction which could have only one conclusion.

Impatiently he pulled at the belt of her robe so that it parted for him, allowing him to reach one hand inside and cup the swollen globe of her breast, and he heard her make some sound midway between a purr and a protest.

'Look down,' he instructed softly, and she obeyed the order instantly, watching his fingertips as they began to softly encircle each tight, rosy nipple, and seismic little shocks of pleasure began to ripple over her.

She reached blindly for the belt of his trousers. Then her fingers scrabbled down like those of a woman possessed as she urgently eased the zip down, feeling the great power of him in the palm of her hand as he sprang free. And she curled her fingers possessively around his silky hardness.

'*Matri di Diu!*' he gasped out, and lowered her gently onto the carpet, unable to wait or to risk moving—like a schoolboy on his first ever encounter with a woman. He began to fumble in the pocket of his trousers.

She could feel him sliding a condom on and then pushing his trousers down, but only down, and she knew then with an erotic certainty which aroused her far more than it shocked her, that he wasn't even going to take them off. That he was going to take her…take her…

Oh, lord—here! *Here!* Distractedly she turned her head to the side as he lowered himself on top of her. The floor-to-ceiling windows were uncurtained, and it was broad daylight. Someone might see!

'Giovanni,' she husked, from a mouth which suddenly felt as dry as sandpaper.

He paused from tugging at her breast with his mouth, teeth

nipping and grazing in an action which veered tantalisingly between pain and pleasure. '*Chi?*' He saw her look of confusion, and realised that he had spoken in Sicilian. 'What is it?' he questioned feverishly.

With a finger which was shaking she pointed at the window, through which strolling couples could be seen ambling along the towpath in the golden summer evening. 'Someone might see us,' she whispered.

Some madness almost made him cry out that he didn't care—such was his urgent need to possess her. But he had never approved of voyeurism.

With a groan he eased himself away from the honeyed lure of her body, and used the opportunity to kick his trousers away, his modesty maintained by the silken shirt which skimmed the tops of his thighs. His shoes and socks followed, and Kate sucked in a frantic breath which did nothing to quell the acceleration of her heart.

He moved around the side of the room, so that he could not be seen from the outside, and drew the curtains together, and in the few short steps back to where she lay, her eyes dark with hunger and excitement, he unbuttoned his shirt halfway and pulled it over his head.

She lay watching him, saw how proud and aroused he was. Pale light filtered through the curtains and transformed him into a glorious dark and golden silhouette, and she thought that she might pass out if he didn't come back to her quickly.

For one moment he towered above her, unsmilingly surveying the beautiful bounty of her body as she stretched out on the backdrop of silver satin.

She thought how cold his face suddenly looked, inappropriately cold considering how much he obviously wanted her, and she felt the skittering fingers of foreboding icing her skin. But she could not stop him. Not now. Certainly not now. She sensed that he still blamed her for seducing him, but none of that seemed to matter. In fact, nothing seemed to matter other than to have him here with her again...

He sank down and edged the robe completely free, easing it off the pale curves of her shoulders, until she was as naked as he was.

He jerked his head arrogantly towards the window. 'Is that private enough for you, *cara*?'

Her desire for him made her ignore everything—even the sardonic tone in which he had asked the question. Greedily her hands went up to his shoulders. And where her fingers led her mouth followed as she anointed the soft olive gleam of his skin with eager, tiny kisses.

She was wild! Giovanni was deadly sober, but he felt almost drunk with a cold, hard power as he parted her legs and touched her syrupy warmth, so that she bucked with pleasure beneath his fingers.

'Oh!' The single syllable came out in an ecstatic little moan.

He reined in his own needs, wanting to see her even more in his power. His hand stilled. 'Oh, what?'

Kate very nearly wept with frustration. 'Please,' she breathed.

'Please what?' he questioned cruelly.

Her pride now vanquished by the clamour of her senses, she whispered, 'Please do it some more,' and was rewarded with a sure instinctive touch that took her to the very edge.

He could make her come right now, beneath his fingers like last time, he thought with a grim kind of satisfaction. But pleasure was all the more intense when it was prolonged. He moved his hand away, unbearably excited by the sulky little pout of her lips.

'Oh!'

'No, no, no, *cara*,' he murmured, enjoying the way she writhed frustratedly beneath him. 'A little while longer. Why not try...*this* instead...?' and without warning he slipped inside her, seeing her eyes dilate as their flesh joined and he filled her.

He moved, slowly at first. Long, deep, agonisingly slow thrusts, and Kate felt so full of him that she felt as though her heart might burst.

He was playing with her, she thought almost bitterly. Demonstrating his control over her, while she, like a puppet, submitted willingly to the orchestrations of his body.

He did not kiss her. Just watched the mindless flutter of her eyes, the way the breath escaped from her parted lips in frenzied little sighs.

'Open your eyes,' he instructed softly.

She did, then almost wished she hadn't—because there was not a single scrap of tenderness etched on that dark, beautiful face. Just a primitive kind of hunger, which she could see he was reining in with an effort. But succeeding. Oh, yes, he was certainly succeeding.

'You have beautiful eyes,' he whispered.

Was he trying to punish her, by making her wait? To pay her back for what he obviously blamed her for—getting him into bed in the first place?

'Tell me what it feels like,' he instructed softly, and thrust deep inside her once more.

'Heaven!' she burst out, before she had time to think about the wisdom of her reply.

He gave a laugh then, a low, soft, mocking sound of triumph, but the triumph backfired on him when she began to move beneath him, changing the pace so irrevocably that he was caught up on an inexorable ascent towards mindless pleasure.

He gave a small moan as he felt power slip away from him, but the unwillingness of his surrender was quickly replaced by the stealthy warmth of abandonment.

Abandonment?

No, even stronger than that. He was a man who had always

lived his life by rules. And structure. So what was happening to him now?

The feeling which rocked him took him completely off-guard, and her own corresponding gasps of pleasure as she spasmed around him made him tip his head back in a disbelieving kind of wonder as he came and came and came, his seed spilling uselessly into the condom.

And then he rolled off her and gazed unseeingly at the ceiling.

He hadn't known it could feel quite like that.

# CHAPTER SEVEN

GIOVANNI must have slept—fallen into an unusually deep, and dreamless, interlude. Only with consciousness did reality begin to chase strange images across his mind.

Red hair and green eyes, and a body which had taken him to paradise and back again. A feeling of powerlessness as he had climaxed. And that, inexplicably, he had found himself actually *resenting* the protection he wore. Had wanted no barrier between him and her slick, beguiling warmth.

He expelled a sigh and stirred, but he did not open his eyes. He needed to realign his thoughts. To work out just where he went from here.

Beside him Kate was awake, though pretending not to be. She had kept watch over him while he slept, like an anxious mother night-watching a fevered child. Only in sleep had his face relaxed. And in orgasm, she reminded herself as a dull warmth began to seep into her satiated blood.

In sleep she had been able to study him with an intensity she was certain he would not have tolerated had he been awake. And the sight of him had been endlessly fascinating.

The hard mouth had softened into a half-smile, giving his face an unthinkable illusion of vulnerability. The dark lashes which framed those dazzling blue eyes had been like two soft, ivory curves brushing the seamless olive of his skin. His jaw held more than a trace of darkness and she found herself wondering if he was the kind of man who had to shave morning *and* evening. Very probably.

She had resisted the desire to stroke a wondering fingertip all over the hard contours of his face—it was so beautiful in repose. She sighed, a sadness washing over her as she closed her eyes with a hopeless kind of yearning.

Giovanni's eyes snapped open and he turned to look at her, unprepared for her wanton loveliness as she lay stretched out on her side facing him, her head pillowed on her arm, with the rich hair spilling all over the pale flesh of her upper body.

So glorious in her nakedness, he thought with a wrench. The long limbs and the tiny waist and the breasts which were so startlingly lush and heavy. Their rosy centres were peaking and he had to stifle the urge to reach out to cup one and gently circle the flat of his hand there. When he touched her he could not think straight, and he needed to think straight.

'Kate?' he said softly.

She effected to stir, and to stretch, carefully composing her face so that he would not see a woman who had been en-slaved—by a man who treated her in such cavalier fashion. 'Hello,' she said, her voice as soft as his, as her eyelids fluttered open.

His blood pounded. *Diu!* One word and he wanted her all over again! All his good intentions fell by the wayside. 'You want that we go to bed?' he asked her lazily, his English unusually fractured by the stir of his senses. 'Or shall we stay here?'

Either, or both. That was what she wanted. Or anything else he cared to offer her. But Kate knew that she badly needed to assert some kind of control over her behaviour. She had been wayward. Overly compliant. He was a proud and arrogant man, who, so far, had only to snap his fingers for her to accede to his will. And wouldn't that only make him prouder, more arrogant still?

She sat up, as much to escape that horizontal scrutiny as to assert herself. 'I need to take a shower,' she said crisply, conveniently neglecting to mention that she had been soaking in a long bath just before his arrival. But that had been before he...before he...

He saw her sudden, swift rise in colour and knew that he could make her change her mind. He sat up, too—so that he was facing her.

'Together?' His voice grew husky. 'I could do with a shower myself.' He felt the urgent throb of need, and looked down at himself, peeling the spent condom off his renewed hardness. 'See what you do to me?' he questioned ruefully.

Oh, yes, she saw. Just what was he planning? she wondered angrily. Another frantic bout of sex in the shower before he disappeared from her life again? She supposed that she should be grateful he hadn't left immediately, and then wondered whether that was why she had kept watch over him—to ensure that he didn't.

No. The reason had been much more fundamental and primitive than an urge to check that he didn't desert her. She had wanted nothing more than to drink in his beauty and to revel in the power of a strong, virile body—which had moved her in a way that no man ever had done before.

She met the provocative taunt in his eyes. 'Boasting, Giovanni?'

She looked proud at that moment, he realised. Proud and defiant as she tilted her chin at him, the green eyes flashing emerald fire. The ache grew. 'I don't need to boast, Kate,' he mocked. 'And if there is any boast to be made then it should be yours, not mine—for you are the one responsible for my growing desire, *cara*.'

'Because I'm here?' she challenged, deliberately averting her eyes from just how much his desire was growing. 'Would any woman do if I wasn't?'

'Much as I do not wish to pander to your ego,' he retorted softly, 'it might flatter you to know that I have never been unfaithful before.'

'Flatter me?' She let out a short laugh. 'Isn't flattery supposed to include terms of endearment? And you're a little short on those, Giovanni.'

'I never say anything I don't mean,' he answered insolently. 'And extravagant compliments aren't paramount in my mind right now.'

Kate was unprepared for the sharp tang of pain which contracted her heart. 'Thanks a bunch.'

Giovanni looked at her thoughtfully. He had angered her— and what point was there in angering her when he still wanted her so badly? He had put his own anger on hold for that very reason. His disbelief, too—because if he stopped to think about how he had detonated the whole structure of his life because of his inexplicable need for this woman...

No, not need, he told himself fiercely. Desire was not the same as need. 'I told you that you had very beautiful eyes,' he remarked, with a slow smile.

He had also said some fairly comprehensive things about her breasts and her long legs—but shuddered comments about her physical attributes at the height of passion did not constitute endearment. Not in Kate's book. 'Quickly! Let me go and write it down before I forget!' she said sarcastically, and then her senses flared into life again as he reached his hand out to cup her chin.

'Kate,' he said softly. 'Why are we arguing after what we have just shared together?'

She bit her lip. Should she be silent and passive? Or let him know what was *really* on her mind? Thinking that she didn't have a lot to lose, she said quietly, 'We've shared very little except for sex, Giovanni—'

'Exceptionally good sex,' he demurred.

The best. The very best—but sex wasn't what she was talking about. She wanted more than that, unrealistic though it might be. 'Sex isn't everything.'

'No, but it's a pretty big part of everything.' And it had

taught him just what he had been missing... 'What else did you have in mind?' he countered coolly.

She saw his face close and heard his voice become remote. The very last thing she wanted was to come over as some clinging vine. She had given herself to him freely, so she had no right to play the blushing virgin now.

She gave a shrug, as though she hadn't really thought about it, as though she didn't really care one way or the other. 'To sit and have talked over dinner some time might have been nice.'

He didn't know what he had been expecting, but her use of the past tense both intrigued and tantalised him. He had come here today wanting this. Knowing that she would give him this. And had thought that one more time in her arms would be enough. That afterwards he would be able to think of her as nothing more than a bitter-sweet memory. But he had been wrong. It hadn't been enough—no way near enough. 'You're making it sound as though it's over, Kate.'

'Over?' She stared into his blue eyes with genuine surprise. 'Oh, come on, Giovanni—it never really began, did it?'

'Not in the most conventional of ways, no,' he agreed, and Anna's pain swam uncomfortably into the forefront of his mind. 'But surely that doesn't rule out it carrying on?'

'But you live in Sicily, and I live in London,' she pointed out, even as some kind of delirious kind of hope flared into life inside her.

His eyes narrowed imperceptibly. Surely she couldn't be *that* naïve? She was an independent woman who was clearly at ease with her own sexuality; surely she must know how these things worked?

'I wasn't talking about dating,' he said roughly.

The flare of hope was extinguished, but she kept her expression of interest quite steady. 'Oh? Then how are we supposed to ''carry on'', as you put it?'

'I could take a couple of weeks off work,' he told her softly. 'Call my secretary and have her cancel all my engagements.'

And maybe in a way it would be best to absent himself from Sicily. Before he had left for London he had told Anna to damn his name as much as it gave her satisfaction to do so. He knew that he deserved it. But Anna had shaken her smooth, dark head and looked at him with sad eyes as she told him that she would say nothing bad about him. That a man she had loved and wanted to share the rest of her life with could not have suddenly become a villain overnight.

That had been the worst part of all. He had seen her attitude change from one of bitter hurt to one of sweet generosity and an attempt at understanding and forgiving what had happened. And he had recognised in that moment just what had motivated the change. Anna didn't want it to be over, he realised. She was telling him what she thought he wanted to hear, in the hope that he would go back to her. Tacitly, she was telling him that many, many women turned a blind eye to their men's transgressions, and many men revelled in this and exploited it. But Giovanni had just discovered he was not one of them.

He had betrayed Anna, and in so doing, it had made him realise what was missing from his relationship. He had also betrayed the fundamental trust on which their relationship had been based. And the relationship had floundered.

And all because of the naked woman who sat before him, her smooth, high bottom resting indolently on silver satin. She had tempted him and he had succumbed. She had offered him forbidden fruit and he had eaten it. A pulse began to patter at his temple.

'So how about I do that?' he murmured, trying by sheer force of will to deny the heat in his loins. 'Stay around for a couple of weeks and you can show me London.'

Two weeks! He certainly wasn't offering her anything in

the way of permanence, was he? She saw how one hard, hair-roughened thigh had come up to shield his manhood from her, but not before she had seen how aroused he had become. She thought women weren't supposed to get turned on by that kind of thing, but Kate found that she was. Very.

'You want me to show you London?' she asked unsteadily.

She must know how these games were played. He doubted if she would want to hear the unvarnished truth—that he wanted to lose himself in her body for just as long as it took for the fire to leave his veins.

'I'd love you to show me London,' he smiled.

It was the smile that did it. The first real smile she had ever seen curve his lips into an irresistible invitation. If he smiled like that he could ask her to show him around a municipal car-park and she would have thoroughly enjoyed every minute of it.

'I think that can be arranged.' She smiled back at him prettily. 'Where are you staying?'

He frowned. Again, so naïve—or was that all some kind of act? She was, he guessed, around twenty-seven, though she seemed to have honed her sexual prowess to resemble a woman in her forties.

He went for broke. 'Usually I stay at the Granchester—unless you're offering me a bed here, Kate?'

Then she understood what he was getting at. This was a game to be played, an erotic and exciting game. She pretended to consider it, while her heart raced. 'It would make more sense, certainly,' she said slowly. 'Otherwise, I'd just have to pick you up from the hotel every morning, wouldn't I?'

His blue eyes flashed. 'Of course it all depends…'

'On what?'

Another smile. A more predatory smile this time. Much more predatory. 'On how many bedrooms you have.'

She struggled to adopt an insouciant air, even as she felt the honeyed rush of desire. 'Just the one.' She swallowed.

'Oh. That decides it, then. I'll arrange to have my bags sent over from the hotel.' He gave a dark smile which sent shivers down her spine. 'But let us waste no more time talking of accommodation, Kate,' he murmured. 'Didn't you say something about taking a shower?'

She framed her lips to say 'alone', then shut them again. He was here. For two weeks. As her lover. She gave a shiver of anticipation. Why bother denying herself what she most wanted?

She rose elegantly to her feet and stared down at him, the raw look of approbation which he washed over her making her revel in her nakedness. 'Will you wash my back for me, Giovanni?' she questioned innocently.

Heat flooded him, and he snaked his hand around her ankle, whispered his fingertips up behind her knee to her inner thigh, and then found her where she was still as molten moist as before. Kate's knees gave way and she sank back down to the carpet.

'The shower?' she said weakly and she saw the look of dark intent on his face as he reached for the packet of condoms once more.

'Will wait,' he growled, and began to kiss her.

# CHAPTER EIGHT

KATE got her shower in the end, and so did Giovanni, because he joined her, just as he had said he would, and she found herself wondering whether this was a man who always got exactly what he wanted.

She had never had a shower like it in her life and she had never given herself so freely to a man before. It was as though she was powerless to do anything other than to react to the mastery of his body.

He slowly soaped every bit of her—indecently slowly, so that she heard herself moaning in protest beneath his touch. His fingers lingered on her breasts, and on the tiny swell of her belly, before sliding in between her thighs to bring her to a shuddering orgasm right there in the shower.

Then it was her turn. She stroked her way over his firm flesh, heated by a renewed need herself as he sprang into vibrant life beneath her fingertips.

His eyes glittered as he realised what she was trying to do. 'No,' came the silken rebuttal, before he lifted her up to thrust into her over and over again, while her legs straddled him, her soft thighs pressing into the hard jut of his hips.

'Giovanni!' she gasped.

'That's my name,' he agreed in a grim kind of voice, uncharacteristically feeling himself teetering on the brink of control, and resenting it even as he gloried in it. His mouth hardened as he reined in his desire.

Kate had never been made love to in a shower before, and the contrast between his hot, hard entry and the gushing water that flooded down on them only seemed to intensify her pleasure. She would have liked him to kiss her, but the confined space made kissing difficult. Maybe he liked that, she thought with a sudden wave of sadness—because kissing brought with it a certain kind of tenderness; but then he drove into her even harder and thought gave way to pure, beautiful sensation.

She opened her mouth at the moment of fulfilment and warm water rained into it, at the very same time as Giovanni dissolved with a low, rasping moan of completion.

His face looked darkly serious as he lifted her away from him, the blue eyes giving nothing away.

'Are you always this generous a lover, *cara*?' he asked sombrely, the deep voice sounding almost shaken.

She hid her face by bending to pick up the soap, which had flown from someone's grip—hers or his, she couldn't remember. His question seemed to imply that she carried on like this with hundreds of men—oh, if only he knew how small was the number of lovers in her life!

'I hope so,' she prevaricated, and saw his mouth tighten.

He wondered why it filled him with the white-hot heat of fury to imagine her like this with another man. Why should he have unrealistic expectations of a woman like this?

Anna had been a virgin, had known only him as her lover, and he had always held back just a little, for fear of shocking her.

Yet with Kate he was at his most inhibitedly rampant. He couldn't seem to get enough of her. Novelty value, he told himself angrily, that was all it was. Two weeks of non-stop sex should be able to cure him of *that*.

But, in the meantime, they had run out of certain essential supplies.

'Let me wash your hair for you, *cara*,' he coaxed in velvet entreaty. 'And then…'

'Then?' The question came out breathlessly, because, supper forgotten, all she wanted to do was to take him to her bed. What on earth was happening to her?

'We need to go out.'

'Out?' she pouted.

He gave a low laugh, and ran his finger over the swollen contours of her mouth, the laugh becoming one of delight when she nipped at the tip with her teeth like a tiny animal. 'Yes, out, my beautiful, wanton Kate.'

'Are you hungry?'

'Very,' he answered truthfully, because he had skipped lunch.

'Well, I have plenty of food in. Champagne, too,' she added hopefully, as an incentive.

He gave an almost imperceptible shake of his head. He did not want to drink champagne with her. Why celebrate a fundamental flaw in his character, which he was only just discovering? That this woman had a certain power over him, that she had taken something from him which he had not intended to give? 'But there is one vital provision we have run out of,' he told her softly.

'What?'

For answer he took her hand and guided it between his legs until it touched the silky surface of the rubber which was still in place.

'We have used three already,' he told her, on a silken boast.

She felt a detached feeling of disappointment as she let her head rest on his wet shoulder. Of course that was all he was thinking of—that was all they had ever shared, wasn't it? 'The chemist it is, then,' she said, her voice muffled against his skin.

But he heard the disappointment, and frowned. He lifted her face and looked down into it, thinking how curiously vulnerable her bare, wet face seemed—and what a contrast to the firebrand she had been in his arms. 'You want to have dinner, don't you?' he said softly. 'So go and get ready. We'll buy what we need and then I'll take you out to eat.'

And Kate was unprepared for the great leap of excitement in her heart as she pulled the shower door open.

It isn't a date, she told herself fiercely as she wrapped a towel round her and walked through to the bedroom. It's just a meal—the fuel we need for what is doubtless going to be a marathon bout of delicious sensation.

But she dressed as if she was going on a date.

The first time she had met him she'd been working—and on the two occasions she had seen him since she had been surprised by him at the flat. Tonight she had been wearing nothing but a satin robe and there had been no opportunity to prepare herself, to make sure that she looked her best.

Now was her opportunity to pull all the stops out. To dazzle and beguile him. He might only be here for two weeks, and he might only want her as his temporary lover—but he would see her looking her very best!

She pulled a black dress from her wardrobe, a dress she rarely wore—because it always seemed a little too 'grown-up' for her. But tonight she wanted to feel grown-up—a real woman, in the company of a real man.

It was the simplest dress imaginable—a shift of jet linen—and the beauty was all in the cut. It had cost her a small fortune, and it showed—especially when she scraped her hair back into an almost severe chignon, which meant that her face looked all eyes, fringed with an extravagant lashing of mascara.

She wore no jewellery—the moonstones seemed all wrong, somehow, and she possessed no 'real' jewellery. With her long, slim legs encased in dark silk stockings, the final touch was a pair of outrageous little black shoes with kitten heels.

Giovanni sat waiting for her in the sitting room, his hair still damp from the shower. She saw that he had brought up his bags from the car, and was wearing a snowy-white shirt and some dark, amazing trousers, and the blue eyes were watching her every movement as she swayed into the room.

He pursed his lips and let out an exaggerated long, low whistle of appreciation.

'Mmm,' he murmured. '*Bella.*'

But if she had hoped for kisses now she was to be disappointed, for he made no move to touch her.

He didn't dare. His swallowed down his desire. She looked absolutely breathtaking in a dress that would have looked outstanding in any company. With her hair off her face like that, she looked almost icy. Unapproachable. And again, the contrast to the woman who had straddled him in the shower minutes earlier was quite devastating. If he touched her he knew exactly what would happen—and what would be the use of removing such a beautiful garment from her body before dinner?

Something in the way he was looking at her made Kate feel suddenly unsure of herself. This really was the most bizarre situation, she thought. She had been more intimate with him than she had with any other man, and yet she didn't have a clue what was going on in his mind. 'You like it, then?' she asked him unnecessarily.

A muscle flickered at his cheek. 'You know I do.'

But still he kept his distance. She pinned a bright smile onto her mouth. 'It's getting late; shall we go?'

'Sure.'

Outside, the evening sun danced golden on the river, and they began to walk towards the shops and restaurants.

'Shall we eat first?' he asked.

At least he had given her the choice. It seemed almost too clinical to go and stock up at the pharmacy while they walked side by side as if they were two strangers. Intimate strangers. 'Yes, please,' she answered gratefully.

He heard the relief in her voice. 'And where are you going to take me?'

'I haven't decided yet.'

She didn't take him to her favourite restaurant. They knew

her by name there, and she had no desire for them to get to know Giovanni, too. They might jump to all kinds of the wrong conclusions and think that he was a proper boyfriend. And she wasn't sure she could face the awkward questions which would be bound to arise when he disappeared from her life as suddenly as he had entered it.

Instead, they found a small Indian eaterie which had received rave reviews in the national Press. The place was teeming and a table looked unlikely, but the *maître d'* took one glance at the imposing Sicilian and the pale-faced woman at his side and immediately summoned them in to a small table in one corner of the room.

It was, Kate realised as she sat down to face him, the first time that they had done anything 'normal' together—unless you counted that first, awkward lunch at his godmother's. It didn't help that her hands were shaking as she took the menu, but how could she not feel a trembling bag of nerves? He looked *adorable*. Outrageously good-looking and confident.

She couldn't miss the side-looks which most of the other female diners gave him, followed by envious glances in *her* direction. I don't want to adore him, she told herself. An emotion like that would be wasted on a relationship that wasn't going anywhere past the bedroom.

'I hope you like Indian food?' she questioned conventionally.

His appetite, peculiarly, had deserted him, but he forced a bland smile. 'I'm not familiar with it.' The sapphire gaze captured her. 'Perhaps you would like to order for me?'

She nodded, suspecting that he rarely let a woman take control. 'OK.' She scanned the menu with uninterested eyes.

She didn't have a clue what she was ordering, even though she loved Indian food with a passion. She just jabbed her finger indiscriminately at the menu and hoped for the best.

'We should drink beer with curry,' she told him when she had ordered the drinks.

'So you've changed your mind about champagne?' he drawled.

She looked up from the menu, her heart thudding painfully in her chest. 'We haven't really got anything to celebrate, have we?'

Was it another sudden look of vulnerability that made him say it? 'Except for the most erotic afternoon of my life,' he answered softly.

'Mine, too,' she admitted helplessly.

'So far,' he added, and the soft blue gleam from his eyes set her pulses racing.

She stared at him, trying to see beyond the dark glamour of his looks and the lazy sophistication he exuded. 'Listen,' she sighed, 'we can't spend the whole evening talking about sex, can we?'

He laughed. 'Well, we *can*.... I think what you mean to say is that it could become rather wearing.'

'Thanks for the language lesson,' she responded drily, taking a sip from the glass of lager which the waiter put on the table in front of her.

'What do you want to talk about?' he murmured. 'You want to tell me a little something of your life?'

Again she tried to pretend that this was a normal first date, but her words came out in a stilted list of facts. 'My parents live on the outskirts of London. One older sister. Her name is Lucy.'

'And where is she?'

'She lives in the flat below mine.'

He raised his eyebrows. 'So, two successful, affluent sisters living close to one another—how pleased your parents must be.'

'Yes. They are.' But she didn't want to talk about herself—she wanted to learn about this man to whom she had given herself so freely. She looked at him curiously. 'Your English is absolutely brilliant.'

'There you go again,' he murmured, recognising a deliberate attempt to change the subject. 'Stereotyping me.'

'I wasn't!' she protested.

'Yes, you were!' His faint accent became suddenly exaggerated and pronounced, like a caricature of a foreign accent. 'You want me to talk like *theese, cara*?'

She laughed, but the stupid thing was that his voice sent shivers up and down her spine, no matter *which* way he talked.

She shook her head. 'Tell me where you learnt to speak it so well.'

'In America.'

So *that* explained the accent. *And* the fluency.

'I lived there—for a year in between leaving college and starting work in the company,' he explained, shrugging his shoulders in answer to the question in her eyes. 'My father thought it wise to become completely fluent before I did so. It can be such a disadvantage to have to negotiate in a foreign language unless you are completely familiar with it. People can try to take you for a fool,' he finished, on an odd kind of note.

'I can't imagine anyone trying to take *you* for a fool,' she said slowly.

His eyes glittered. He wondered if she had any idea just how irresistible her mouth was. 'If that was a compliment, then I thank you.'

'Just an observation,' she returned lightly and put her glass of lager down. 'So what was life like in America?'

He sighed. He had worked hard and partied hard, and during the process had come into contact with many beautiful women who had made no secret of their attraction for the tall, lean Sicilian with the disconcerting blue gaze. But despite the attractions not once had he succumbed to any of *their* undoubted charms.

He had been dating Anna since his third year in college,

and had recognised that in her he had found a woman who would make him the perfect wife. Through the many years which had followed, that certainty had never wavered. And yet he had thrown it all away for Kate Connors.

'It was exactly as you would expect,' he said coolly. 'Very vast and very different to the land I had grown up in.'

She heard the edge to his tone and wondered wildly whether a getting-to-know-you dinner had been such a good idea after all. Were they destined only to be compatible when they were horizontal? How about the easy conversation she *usually* managed to achieve when she was in the company of an intelligent, attractive man? She struggled for the right, light touch, even as she despised her own eagerness to please him. 'But you liked it?'

He shrugged. 'It was a new experience—and experience is always useful.'

She gave him a frozen smile. 'And is that how you categorise me, Giovanni? As a useful experience?'

He gave her question a moment's consideration. 'Not just as a useful experience, no.' His eyes mocked her as he lifted his glass in a toast. 'More as a rather beautiful and enjoyable one. Wouldn't you agree?'

But it sounded more of a boast than a tribute, and Kate was glad that their food arrived at that precise moment, and that the ladling out of rice and chicken and lentils occupied their hands as well as meaning that she could drop her eyes from that unsettling gaze.

She wanted to ask him more about his life in order to find out more about the man, but she was scared of what it might reveal. His history would inevitably include details of his engagement, now broken—which instinct told her he bitterly regretted and blamed her for, at least in part. Because, despite his outwardly relaxed air, there was an unmistakable tension about him, a repressed kind of anger which he was only just managing to conceal.

She forced herself to eat a mouthful of curry, while he seemed to have no such reservations, eating his food with a sensual enjoyment, which was a pleasure to watch. And she found herself wishing that she had not been so compliant from the outset, wondering if she had applied her usual brakes something more enduring than a two-week affair might have come of it.

He glanced up to find her looking at him. She had barely touched a thing. 'You're not hungry?'

She made a play of eating a piece of chicken, then put her fork down. 'Not really.'

'You want to leave?'

'When you've finished.'

He ate a last mouthful of rice, his blue eyes fixed thoughtfully on hers. Then he put his own fork down and reached his hand across the table to take hers. 'You're not having second thoughts, are you, Kate?' he questioned softly, unprepared for the sudden jolt of disappointment as he imagined her saying yes.

Of course she was. But even third or fourth thoughts wouldn't make her change her mind. Not now. She gave her head a little shake, even managing a little smile. 'Of course not,' she told him serenely as he raised his hand to call for the bill. It was a little late for that!

Outside, he took her hand as they walked slowly back to the flat, stopping off at the pharmacy on the way.

And Giovanni looked at her with an expression of bemusement lighting his blue eyes when he had seen her rise in colour as he had taken his wallet out to pay for his purchase.

'Why, Kate,' he observed softly, running a fingertip across her hot cheek, 'you're blushing.'

She wanted to tell him that this wasn't the kind of thing she normally did—but what was normal any more? He probably wouldn't believe a word of it, and why should he? 'They know me in this shop,' she said drily, by way of explanation.

'Then they will know that you choose your lovers wisely,' he returned with an irresistible glitter of his eyes.

And all her doubts were driven away at the first hungry touch of his lips once the door of her flat had closed behind them.

'I want you,' he told her unsteadily.

'I'm right here,' she whispered back.

The next morning Kate rang downstairs and had Lucy clear her diary for the next two weeks, and launched whole-heartedly into a fairy-tale, unreal romance.

It was her first experience of living with a man—though the term 'living' had a sort of permanence about it which didn't quite ring true in this case.

She set aside a shelf in the bathroom for him, and cleared a space in her wardrobe for his suits. She learned that he liked nothing more than black coffee for breakfast, that opera pleased him more than any other kind of music and that whatever emotions he had—and sometimes she wondered— he kept them firmly locked away on the inside. For Kate had only ever seen him angry—or passionate when he took her in his arms. The cool Giovanni who accompanied her to restaurants and art galleries—he gave nothing away.

Two days after he had first moved in, he met Lucy.

Kate had been dreading the meeting, without really knowing why, but one look at the disapproval which Lucy iced at him was enough to tell her that her fears had been justified.

'Your sister doesn't like me,' he observed after Lucy had said a stilted hello and refused coffee.

'She doesn't know you,' answered Kate brightly.

'OK, she doesn't approve of me, then.' He paused and looked at her. 'And why should that be, Kate?'

She supposed that there was no point in lying. She sighed. 'She knows about you, and the fact that you were engaged when we first met,' she added, in answer to the questioning look in his eyes.

'And your sister, being such a paragon of virtue, naturally disapproved, did she? What does she do for a living, just out of interest—other than glare at your houseguests?'

Kate suppressed a shudder at his choice of word. House-guest. You couldn't get any more coldly unemotional than that, could you? 'She works for me. She takes and makes bookings, does my accounts, answers the phone—that kind of thing. And there's no need to make it sound as though I have houseguests like *you* all the time!'

'And do you?' he drawled insolently, but the knife-edge of jealousy twisted itself sharply in his gut.

Bitter reproach sparked green fire from her eyes. 'What do you think?'

He drove the jealousy away and forced himself to stay calm. 'I'd like to think that this was a one-off situation,' he told her steadily. 'For you as much as for me.'

'For your ego's sake, I suppose?' she questioned heatedly.

He shook his dark head. 'No, Kate, more for my pride's sake.'

'Oh, really?'

'And yours too, of course.'

'Oh, you're…you're…'

He gave a soft laugh as he acknowledged her fire. 'What am I, *cara*?'

'Impossible!' she declared, without really knowing why. Or maybe she did. Maybe her rage was directed more at the fact that he would never really be hers to have—other than in a particularly satisfying, but curiously empty, sexual sense. Angrily she turned away from him, but he reached a lazy hand out and stopped her, pulling her, still resisting, into his arms. She struggled a little. 'Go away!' she stormed as he bent to brush his lips against hers.

'You know you don't mean that,' he murmured, feeling their velvet surface begin to tremble at that first contact.

'Yes, I do…. *Oh!*'

He kissed her in earnest then, and she went under, only to gaze up at him dazedly when eventually he stopped the kiss. 'That wasn't fair,' she whispered as she met the question in his eyes.

'What wasn't?'

'You say outrageous things to me and then think you can just kiss them better!'

'So what do you want me to stop doing, *cara*—saying the outrageous things, or kissing them better?'

His cajoling tone coaxed her lips into an unwilling smile. 'What do you think?' she asked, and he tipped her face up to trap her in a blinding blue stare, a different kind of question in his eyes this time.

'I think we'd better go back to bed and make up properly, don't you?' he questioned unsteadily.

'But we've only been up an hour!' Her protest sounded feeble even to her own ears, and the look of hungry intent on his face had her babbling at him like a tour-guide, watching in reluctant fascination as he smiled the smile of a man who knew he had won the battle. 'And we were going to go to visit the Tower of London today, remember?'

'It's been standing there for centuries; it'll wait for a few more hours,' he told her arrogantly, and led her back towards the bedroom.

# CHAPTER NINE

'I THINK that's everything.' Giovanni clicked shut his suitcase, and turned to look at where she stood, silently surveying him, her face impassive, and he wondered what thoughts were going through that beautiful head of hers.

So far, at least, there had been no word or demonstration that Kate was going to miss him, after a fortnight spent almost exclusively together—save when she had made an excuse to go downstairs to see her sister to discuss work.

And Kate watched him with a dull ache in her heart. Intellectually she had known that this moment would come, and emotionally she had prepared herself for the inevitable pain it would bring. But the reality was far worse than even her worst imaginings.

'What time does your plane leave?'

He flicked a glance at his watch, and then again at her. 'In two hours.' If it had been at any other time during the past two weeks then he might have tried to make love to her one more time. But this goodbye was turning into something he hadn't quite anticipated, and to take her into his arms to lose himself in that mindless pleasure would, he knew, somehow devalue what they had shared together.

'Would you like some coffee before you go?'

More in an attempt to dissolve the brittle atmosphere than because he really wanted a cup, he nodded in agreement. 'Please.'

She busied herself in the kitchen. Best cups. Best coffee. Some outrageously expensive chocolate biscuits she had once been given and which there had never been a right time to open. Before now.

She spooned coffee into the cafetiére and stared sightlessly out of the window. Would she ever have agreed to this arrangement if she had known that the inevitable parting would prove so painful?

When she carried the tray back into the sitting room he was half sitting, half lying on the sofa watching her, and her heart leapt as it always did at the sight of him.

'Smells good,' he remarked.

'Mmm.' She wished he would *say* something, other than make those bland comments which could have come from a stranger, and not the man who had shared her life for the past fortnight. She handed him a cup and then took her own over to the opposite side of the room and placed it on a small table beside her.

The distance between them seemed to be the size of a tennis court.

'Kate,' he said suddenly. 'Come and sit next to me.'

Her eyes narrowed and she felt the lurch of disappointment. Physical closeness meant only one thing where they were concerned. 'There isn't time, Giovanni,' she told him dully, unprepared for the tightening of his mouth in response.

'You think that the only reason I want you beside me is so that I can make love to you one more time before I go!' he accused hotly. 'Is that it?'

'There's no need to sound so outraged! That's what it always *does* mean where you're concerned!' she told him. 'And we've hardly been behaving like saints for the last couple of weeks, have we?'

'No.' He put his coffee down untouched, and got up to look out of the window, his hands thrust deep inside his pockets as he stared out at the river which was made silvery-grey by the rain today.

Kate watched the tense set of his shoulders and then he turned round, his face looking as though he was fighting some kind of inner war with himself.

'It doesn't have to be over you know, Kate.'

It was her wildest dream become glorious reality. 'What do you mean?' she questioned slowly, and her heart seemed to deafen her with its pounding.

'You know that I come back to England from time to time?' Kate stilled as his words began to make immediate sense.

'Go on,' she said in a strangled kind of voice. 'Explain exactly what it is I think you're suggesting.'

He was trying to think logically about what would work best. For both of them. He gave a slow smile, captivating her with that mocking blue stare. 'I can make sure that business brings me here on Friday—maybe I could stay over until Sunday. Here, with you.' The smile grew lazier. 'How does that sound, *cara*?'

She thought of snatched weekends of bliss with him. Perfect, but never enough. It never *could* be enough. She would be transformed into one of those bloodless women who lived their whole lives from phone call to phone call. The odd visit would dominate her life, until the rest of it grew indistinct and she would become one of those 'nearly' women. Nearly living, but not quite.

She shook her head. 'Thanks, but no, thanks.'

He felt a flicker of irritation only marginally greater than the one of surprise. He had been confident enough in his power over her to expect her to accept. 'Not even a moment to consider it, Kate?' he questioned sardonically.

'I don't need to consider it.'

'May I ask why?'

'It's not what I want from a relationship, Giovanni.'

'What exactly do you object to?' he drawled.

It hurt that he couldn't see. 'All the highs of infrequent passion aren't enough.' She shrugged. 'It isn't *real*, don't you see?'

A muscle began to pulse in his cheek. 'I haven't heard you doing any complaining!'

She withered him a look. 'That was different. That was never planned to be anything other than short-term, was it? The terms were laid out very carefully at the beginning. Surely you can't have forgotten?'

But he had been certain that he would want to let go by now, and he had been wrong. For a man who was rarely wrong it had been a salutary experience. His anger had been spent, but not so his passion for her—that raged like the fierce storm it had always been. He drew a deep breath, knowing that this was as close to conciliation as he would get.

'Look, just what do you want, Kate?' he said evenly. 'We still haven't known each other very long. Surely you're not holding out for living together—'

Her sharp, outraged intake of breath halted him.

'I am *not*,' she said icily, 'holding out for *anything*! My life is not a game show, Giovanni—even though sometimes it's felt weird enough to be one during the last couple of weeks—'

'And just what is *that* supposed to mean?' Now it was his turn to sound icy.

How could she tell him that whatever he gave her, it was never enough? That she wanted more, and more still. She needed to go deeper with him than the great sex and the lunches and dinners and trips around London. She wanted more than a surface relationship, and she could not have it, she realised. Not with him.

'Nothing, Giovanni.' She gave a weary sigh as she raked her fingers to pull the fall of hair back from her face, and looked at him sadly. 'I knew it had to end, and so did you. I just don't want it to end on a bad note.' She hesitated. 'But neither do I want to try to sustain something we both know isn't sustainable.'

'So that's it?'

'It doesn't have to be this way. We can say goodbye, and enjoy the memories of what we had.'

His face grew even more shuttered. 'As you wish.' He walked across the room and picked up his bags. 'But you'll forgive me if I don't hang around.'

'Of course,' she said stiffly, but she followed him out to the front door all the same, opening it for him and praying that he would kiss her. One last kiss to remember him by.

And, looking down at her, he knew what she wanted. Oh, yes. They had kept areas of their lives out of bounds for necessary reasons of survival. They had not discussed Anna, or the man she herself had been briefly engaged to. Those topics would have caused pain and jealousy and recriminations.

But her physical needs he knew inside out. He knew her body and her desires almost better than he knew his own. Not to kiss her would be to punish her, and a cruel and ruthless streak badly wanted to punish her for her rejection of him. Except that he needed that kiss just as badly as she did.

Something to remember her by.

He dropped the bags and drew her into his arms, and her eyes closed as though she could not bear to read what was in his face.

He kissed her. Softly at first, and then with a growing ardour which he knew he must quell, and when he pulled away from her, almost violently, they both gave ragged little sighs of regret.

As her eyelids fluttered open she was unsurprised by the hard and uncompromising set of his features, knowing that he could offer her nothing more than the very bare essentials.

She heard her lips framing a question she had not intended to ask. 'And will you see...Anna?'

She wanted a reassurance that he was unwilling or unable

to give her. What the hell did she expect him to do? Renounce all others out of some inappropriate loyalty to a woman who had just said she didn't want to see him again?

'Of course,' he said, quietly and truthfully, and saw how she tried not to let her pain show. 'Sicily is a small island. We share many friends—it is inevitable that I shall see her.'

She wanted to ask him whether he would rekindle his engagement, whether absence had changed his feelings about Anna, but she didn't dare. She was afraid of what the answer might be. She nodded instead. 'Goodbye, Giovanni,' she whispered.

'*Ciao, bella*,' he gritted and swung out of the door before he could change his mind.

He fumed all the way to the airport, and thought how ironic it was that he remained angry, when he had sought her out precisely to rid himself of that emotion. And for two weeks he had existed in a state which had pushed that anger to the recesses of his mind, but now it was back, and with a brand-new focus.

So why was he angry now? Because she had told him that she had no wish to continue the affair? Wasn't his Sicilian pride wounded more than his heart?

Very probably.

It was purely physical, he told himself grimly as he returned his car to the hire company and picked up his bags. All it ever was and all it ever could be.

He followed the signs to the departure lounge, telling himself that he would fly home and forget all about her.

'Can I get you anything, sir?'

'Mmm?' He looked up absently.

'Some coffee perhaps? Or something else?'

The stewardess flashed him the kind of smile which told him that there was more than coffee on offer, should he so desire.

Enjoy your freedom, he told himself. *Enjoy* it!

'Coffee would be perfect,' he drawled in Italian, and allowed the corners of his mouth to lift in a smile which made the woman's eyes dilate with undisguised pleasure.

And he sank down into the comfort of the First Class lounge, while the stewardess fussed round him like a hen.

After he had gone, Kate behaved like a woman bereaved—not wailing or crying, but going from room to room to try to hang on to what she had left of him before it disappeared forever.

The scent of him on her pillow, and on the towel which she fished out of the laundry basket. Even his half-drunk cup of coffee she foolishly felt like preserving. But soon the pillowcase and the towel would go into the washing machine, and the cup in the dishwasher and then there would be no trace at all left of him—save the red roses he had bought her last week, and which were already beginning to wilt.

She buried her face in the flowers. Their bloom was fast-fading but the petals were still velvety-soft, and there remained the last sweet, lingering trace of scent. She breathed in deeply, as though that could bring new life to her, but the pleasure she gained was only fleeting, and she wondered how long the dull ache in her heart would last.

She sat staring at the bouquet for a long, long time, and only when she thought that the threat of wayward tears was safely at bay did she pick up the telephone to speak to her sister.

'Hello?'

'Kate?' Her sister's voice immediately filled with concern. 'What's happened?'

'Oh, Lucy,' she said, in an odd, flat voice which didn't sound like her voice at all. 'He's gone.'

'I'm on my way up!' said her sister grimly.

Determinedly Kate stripped the bed while she waited for her sister, and assigned all the temptations of the dirty linen to the laundry basket—because what good would it do her to mope around after him and keep reminding herself of him? That would have only served a purpose if he was coming back.

And he wasn't.

When Lucy arrived, she frowned. 'Are you OK?' The frown deepened. 'Stupid question. Of course you're not OK.'

Kate bit her teeth into her bottom lip. 'Is it too early for wine, do you think?' she asked huskily.

'Nope! In fact you look as though you could use a drink,' said Lucy and followed her out into the kitchen. 'So tell,' she said, still in that same grim voice, 'just what your Sicilian stud had to say for himself before he left!'

'Please don't call him that,' said Kate crossly as she took a bottle of white wine from the fridge and pulled the cork out.

Lucy glared. 'Still protecting him, are you, Kate—even though he's treated you like a concubine for the past fortnight?'

Kate shook her head. 'He has treated me beautifully over the past fortnight,' she defended, her voice softening with memory. 'And I walked into it with my eyes wide open. I wanted it just as much as he did.'

'Well, I hope it was worth it,' said Lucy, accepting the proffered glass.

Kate sipped and thought about it. Had it been? 'I don't know,' she said honestly. 'All I know is that I couldn't resist it—him—at the time, and yet it wasn't enough to carry on with.'

'But you weren't given that option, were you?'

Kate gave a small, rather bitter laugh. 'Actually, I was. Giovanni offered to carry on the affair—with him taking the occasional trip to England and us making a weekend of it.'

'The *bastard*!'

Kate shrugged. 'Not really; you can't blame him for try-ing—'

'Kate, will you stop being so damned *understanding*?'

Kate put her glass down with a shaking hand and turned to look at her sister with tears threatening to spill out of her eyes. 'What alternative do I have?' she whispered. 'At least this way I can remember it with fondness. If I call him every name under the sun—won't that just make everything that we shared seem worthless?'

Lucy shot her a look of understanding. 'You seem to really *like* him.'

Kate shook her head. 'I don't know if *like* is a word you would use in connection with Giovanni—he isn't a man it's easy to get close to. I don't know if there's a word in the dictionary to describe the way I feel about him.'

'Well, if that's the case, why *didn't* you plump for what he was offering you?'

Kate bit her lip. It wouldn't make sense if she told her sister he would lose all respect for her if she opted for the continuation of the affair—because Lucy probably thought that Giovanni had zero respect for her anyway. And she couldn't blame her. Viewed from the outside, she must look like the world's biggest fool—letting a man like that into her home and her life and her heart on a purely temporary basis.

Because something *had* happened during that brief, blissful stay. He had been reluctant to leave, and had shown it this morning, and she wanted to treasure his reluctance for the rest of her life. Surely she must have touched a tiny part of him, for him to have behaved like that?

But she knew that a long-term affair with a man like Giovanni would eventually end, and end bitterly, too—of that she was certain. And she would have her heart broken com-pletely—whilst at the moment it felt only slightly wounded.

Her emerald eyes were brimming with fresh tears as she looked at her sister. 'The affair just wouldn't have been enough,' she told her simply, and Lucy nodded in comprehension.

'Oh, I see,' she said slowly. 'Now I *do* see.' She gave a wry smile. 'But you were wrong, you know, Kate.'

Kate stared at her. 'What are you talking about?'

'There *is* a word in the dictionary to describe the way you're feeling about him.'

Kate's look remained blank.

'It's called love, my darling,' she said gently.

# CHAPTER TEN

THE envelope was waiting for her when she arrived home from work, the writing on it unfamiliar, but with a lurch of her heart Kate guessed exactly who it was from. The elegant, lazy script could only have been penned by one person. She stared at it as if it were an unexploded bomb.

*Open it*, a voice inside her said. Or would a more self-protective woman simply have hurled it into the bin?

She picked it up and slit it open with trembling fingers, and saw that she had been right. Inside was an airline ticket to Barcelona, and a brief, almost insultingly curt note.

—Have three months been enough to change your mind, *cara*? Why not join me in Spain—and we can take up where we left off?

It was signed, 'G'.

She slammed the note down on the table, resisting the stupid urge to read and reread it, to run her eyes hungrily over the two stark sentences again and again.

"Take up where we left off, *indeed*!" And where was that? In bed? Swallowing down her anger and her temptation, she told herself that she would telephone him and tell him exactly what he could do with his ticket.

No. She would ignore it completely—that would be far more effective a refusal. His honour would be outraged! And she wouldn't be susceptible to the honeyed persuasion of his voice.

She kicked her shoes across the sitting room as the telephone started ringing and her heart began to pound uncomfortably. Don't be *crazy*, she told herself. It could be absolutely anyone.

But it wasn't.

She seemed to sense that it was him even before he spoke. There was an infinitesimal, irresistible pause, before she heard him murmur, '*Cara?*'

Sweat broke out in icy pinpricks on her brow. 'I am not your darling!' she snapped.

'No. Not my anything. Not any more,' he agreed mockingly. 'When you will not see me.'

The hardest decision she had ever had to make, but she had stuck by it. 'I meant what I said, Giovanni.'

He sighed. 'I know you did.'

'So why send me a ticket to join you?'

'You know exactly why.' A pause. 'I want to see you.'

'And you're a man who is used to getting what he wants,' she observed.

He didn't answer that. 'Have you missed me?'

'Like a hole in the head!'

There came the sound of soft laughter. 'I don't believe you.'

'That's your prerogative,' she said, but her casual air did not quite come off.

'So you have!'

Yes, she had missed him. Of course she had. She wondered what had ever occupied her mind before she had met Giovanni, because now he seemed to haunt her thoughts constantly. Three months of being away from him, when the minutes and the hours had ticked away with excruciating slowness.

'I'm not coming—'

'Mmm?' he interrupted, on a teasing little note of provocation. 'That cannot be much fun for you, Kate, but I can soon change that, I assure you!'

Her cheeks flamed. 'Giovanni, will you *stop* it!'

'I'm not doing anything,' he protested.

'Yes, you are!'

'What am I doing, *cara*?' he questioned softly.

He was tempting her. Unbearably. Reminding her of how much she had loved being with him, being part of him—even though it had been only a very tiny part. 'I'm going to put the phone down in a minute!' she threatened.

'Wait!' He hesitated, thinking that it was never simple with this woman, and wondering why he did not have the sense to put the phone down himself. 'Come and see me, Kate. Please.'

It was the 'please' that did it—it crept into a heart which she had determinedly steeled against him. Yet that one little word brought all her defences tumbling down like a house of cards. Admit it, she thought to herself—just hearing his voice again was like a soothing balm on a soul which had been tortured and troubled without him.

What was the point of existing in a dull state of misery, when she had the means to make herself happy? Maybe not one hundred per cent happy—but since when did anyone get that? Surely even a little happiness was better than this aching anguish which now seemed second nature to her.

'OK.' Had she *really* said that?

He wondered if he had heard her properly. 'Was that a yes?' he demanded.

'No. It was an OK,' she repeated stubbornly.

He smiled, unseen. *Very* lukewarm, he thought. Almost verging on the sullen—but it was still the surrender he had been intent on. He bit down an instinctive little murmur of triumph, because he sensed that she had been very close to saying no to him. And he wanted her far too much to risk that, though his desire for her still confused him.

Why did her memory persist in possessing him like a fever? he asked himself in silent frustration, as he had been asking himself since he had touched down in Sicily that day three months ago.

He had tried applying logic to a situation where logic seemed redundant. She was beautiful, yes—but he had seen women more beautiful than her.

So was it simply her skills as a lover?

For a while he had tormented himself with the idea that she must have had many, many lovers to be that sensational in bed. To think of her as a whore would make it easy to disregard her. And yet the image had stubbornly refused to stick and, for the life of him, he could not work out why.

'Good,' he said softly. 'You won't regret it, *cara*.'

'I think I'm regretting it already.'

'The flight touches down at eight. I'll be waiting for you, Kate.'

'OK,' she said again, and put the phone down.

She was almost frightened about telling Lucy what she had agreed to, expecting her sister to rage against her and tell her that she must be the most stupid woman on the planet—a sentiment which Kate herself could have sympathy with.

But Lucy surprised her.

'I don't blame you,' she said quietly.

'You *don't*?'

'Uh-uh.'

'Why?'

Lucy shrugged. 'I can see his obvious appeal; men like Calverri don't come along more than once in a lifetime—if you're lucky.'

'Lucky?' echoed Kate, with hollow sarcasm.

'And you've been as miserable as sin since he went away—'

'I haven't—'

'Oh, I know you've *tried* not to be. You've been almost

ridiculously cheerful at times—throwing yourself into your work even more than you usually do, which is saying something! But you've had an air of sadness about you which hurts me to see. So if you're going for a chance of lasting happiness with him—then go for it wholeheartedly.'

But Kate shook her head. 'Not lasting happiness, no—it will be purely temporary. I know that. I'm realistic enough to see that there's no future in it.'

'Then you might ask yourself whether you're just setting yourself up for an even bigger hurt by going. You might be better trying to wean yourself off him for good.'

But she couldn't *not* go—that was the trouble. The thought of seeing him again was making her feel half-mad with the sense of being really and truly alive once more. Just the thought of flying to meet him in Barcelona was like landing in bright sunlight after three months of existing in some kind of shadowland.

She blew a small fortune on new clothes for the trip, telling herself that a shopping expedition was long overdue—she hadn't had the enthusiasm for new clothes since he had gone away. She phoned up the travel agent who told her that the weather would be very warm, but not oppressive.

The flight was smooth and uneventful, but Kate's heart was in her mouth as she walked towards Arrivals, a sudden and debilitating insecurity making her wonder what she would do if Giovanni hadn't bothered to turn up...

She needn't have worried. He was there—of course he was—eclipsing every other person in the vicinity with his presence. Tall and striking, leaning lazily against the barrier. Blue eyes were trained on her like blazing guns, though his expression was as dark and as shuttered as she remembered it.

Kate tried to keep her face calm as she walked towards him, but it wasn't easy—not when she wanted to run at full speed and hurl herself into his arms and tell him how much she had missed him…wanted him…

He was wearing a dark coat of the softest leather imaginable, and it made him look very, very European. More as a distraction from the fact that she didn't know what to say, or how to greet him—for where was the rule-book in a situation like this?—Kate ran her finger along the cuff of the expensive coat.

'This is new,' she observed.

He shimmered his fingertip along the lapel of a sage-green silk jacket, thinking that he had not been expecting such a cool reunion. 'So is this,' he said softly.

His words drew her eyes to his, and once they were locked there she seemed unable to break the gaze.

'Hi,' he murmured.

'Hello,' she said breathlessly.

Her big green eyes drove all conventional greetings clean out of his mind. Oh, what the hell? he thought savagely, and bent his head to kiss her.

'G-Giovanni!' The suitcase fell uselessly from her hand and her fingertips went straight up to his shoulders, biting into the sensually scented leather with an abandon which gathered momentum with each thrust of his tongue as he kissed her with shameless abandon.

'Kate,' he murmured into her mouth, his hand straying irresistibly to the firm swell of her breast, and briefly cupping it in his palm. Until he remembered that they were in a public place, and with an effort he tore his mouth and his hand away.

'*Matri di Diu!*' he swore softly, staring down into the hectic glitter of her eyes. 'I think that we had better go straight to the hotel, don't you, *cara*? Before we are arrested for indecent exposure,' he added, with a low, slightly incredulous laugh.

She supposed that she should be relieved that he wasn't

being hypocritical. Not bothering to dress up the true reason for this weekend together. Straight back to the hotel for two whole nights and very probably two whole days of sensational sex, then back on the plane to London.

And if she had wanted more than what he was offering her she should never have come.

'Sounds wonderful,' she agreed evenly.

Outside the air was warm and soft, and the sky a canopy of indigo velvet, punctured by starlight. He glanced at her as they walked out towards the car. 'You've lost a little weight,' he noticed.

'I needed to.'

'No, you didn't.' He had thought her quite perfect before, but now there was an angular edge to her appearance which made her look like some high-profile model. He saw the side-looks she was getting from the taxi drivers who stood waiting for fares, and instead of feeling a swagger of masculine pride in her beauty he found himself wanting to go and verbally threaten them.

'You're saying that I'm too thin now?'

'A little.' He smiled. 'It will give me enormous pleasure to feed you up, *cara*.' One of many pleasures he anticipated during the days to come.

He settled her into the car, and placed her bags in the back, but thought that she seemed tense as he drove out of the airport towards the hotel.

'Are you OK?' he asked softly.

'Mmm! Just fine,' she answered brightly.

He didn't want her brittle; he wanted her fiery in his arms again. 'Ever been to Barcelona before?' he enquired conversationally as he raced the car towards the city.

She shook her head. 'No, never.' She peered out of the window. 'Do you know it well?'

'Well enough to find my way around without a map.'

Her nerves were making breathing difficult. 'And you're here on business?'

'That's right. A big deal has been concluded.' He shot her a glance, reading nothing in her shadowed profile. 'I have to have dinner with some people tomorrow night. I've known them for years and years.' He indicated right. 'I thought you might like to come along, too?'

'Well, unless you're planning to leave me alone in the hotel for the evening!' she joked, but she felt a surge of satisfaction before reprimanding herself. Just because he wanted to take her out to meet some people he was doing business with didn't mean that they were conducting a normal relationship.

No, her role had been defined from the very beginning: she was his mistress—she gave him pleasure.

And you? mocked an inner voice. Does he give you pleasure, too?

She stole a glance at the hard, dark profile. Of course he did, though she suspected that it had been without any effort on his part. She was almost completely smitten *now*—so imagine what it would be like if he was *trying* to impress her…if he were courting her in a traditional way! But why bother wishing for what she couldn't have? That way led only to disillusionment and heartache.

So snap out of it, she told herself. There was no point in agreeing to come here if she was just going to mope around and wish for the impossible.

She glanced out of the window again. 'So come on, Giovanni,' she murmured, 'let's have the guided tour.'

'My pleasure,' he murmured back, unwittingly echoing her thoughts as he began to tell her about each majestic building they passed.

The hotel was in the Ramblas, close to the enchanting Gothic Quarter of the city, and suitably impressive. He checked her in and then they rode up in the lift towards his suite, but the presence of other guests meant that they stood on opposite sides of the confined space, as awkwardly as strangers.

But the moment he had shut the door behind them, he took her into his arms and began to kiss her, and—whilst part of her wished that he might have waited—she gave herself up to the glory of that kiss. Three months without him became a distant memory as his hard mouth danced sensation all over her skin, and she was shaking and dazed when he finally lifted his head to stare down at her.

'So *did* you miss me?' he questioned silkily.

As a mistress, surely she could be as truthful as she liked. 'I missed *that*,' she admitted.

His mouth hardened. 'And nothing else?'

'My coffee bill has been halved,' she joked and saw the narrowing of his eyes. 'What do you want me to say, Giovanni?' she provoked, half in exasperation. 'That I sat around weeping into my little handkerchief, dreaming of you night after night?'

In her way, her lack of sentiment made it easier to do what he had been almost beside himself with the thought of doing since he had driven away from her flat that morning. His planned offer of a drink forgotten, he ran his hands possessively down the sides of her body, feeling her responding shiver.

'This is how I dreamt of you,' he purred, and shrugged the silk jacket from her shoulders, before tossing it over the back of a chair. 'Like *this*.' With one fluid movement he slid the zip of her skirt down, and as it fell to the floor with a whisper he let out a small, impatient groan when he saw what she was wearing beneath.

A scarlet thong and a matching scarlet garter belt, holding up stockings of creamy white which clung silkenly to the tantalisingly long legs.

'*Matri di Diu!*' he muttered hoarsely.

'You like it?'

'Is it new?' he breathed.

'Mmm.' Kate did her flirty little pirouette, and heard him suck in a ragged breath. She turned round to face him, unprepared for the look of dark, unspoken anger on his face.

'You *don't* like it,' she observed in surprise.

'Who bought it for you?' he demanded.

'What?'

'You heard what I said! A woman does not buy these kind of garments for herself. A man buys these for his mistress!'

'So?' she interjected furiously. 'That's exactly what I am, isn't it?'

'Kate—'

She shook her head in anger. 'Just what *are* you suggesting, Giovanni—that as soon as you got on the plane back to Sicily I replaced you with another stud in my bed?'

Just the thought of it filled him with a murderous rage. 'And did you?'

She very nearly slapped him round the face. 'The fact that you feel the need to ask makes me wonder why I ever agreed to come here,' she told him icily, stooping to retrieve her skirt, but he stayed her, placing his hand on her elbow and gently levering her back up to face him.

'Kate—'

'Take your hands off me,' she said, despising herself for the lack of conviction in her voice.

His voice dropped to a placatory caress. 'I should not have said that, *cara mia*—'

'No, you bloody well shouldn't! If you must know—I bought it...' her voice faltered as she wondered about the wisdom of admitting this '...for you!'

'For me?'

Truthful she was allowed to be, but only up to a point. No need to tell him that if she was going to play the part of mistress then she would play it with a vengeance. And a mistress being reunited with her Sicilian lover would surely wear the finest and flimsiest silk and satin to clothe her body. Delicate garments which she had imagined him slowly or not-so-slowly removing. Garments which would guarantee another invitation for another weekend...

'I'll go and get some big knickers and a plain navy bra if that will make you feel better!' she declared, but he shook his head, and his blue eyes looked almost luminous as he lifted her chin with the tip of his finger.

'Nothing will make me feel better than having you back in my arms again, Kate,' he told her gently. 'Come. Come to me.'

And with a helpless little moan she did exactly that.

He laced his fingers into the thick abundance of her hair and drew her into his body, her warm scent drifting over his senses and igniting their fire. 'I've missed you,' he murmured.

'Honestly?'

'Of course. Do you imagine that you are easy to forget?'

She felt his hands slide from her hair to cup the smooth globes of her bottom, and she gave a little cry. She had missed him, too—but she certainly wasn't going to tell him how much.

Because mistresses did not make such statements of ardour and commitment. That tended to scare the object of their affection away. Instead, she began to unbutton his shirt. 'There's a time for talking,' she said shakily.

'And that time isn't now,' he agreed, his eyes closing as her questing fingers found his nipples and began to stroke enticing little circles.

It took him precisely ten seconds to remove her clothes.

'You've hardly noticed all my new finery!' she complained as the bra slithered off to join the skirt.

'Another time! I want to see you naked,' he ground out,

his breath hot and urgent as it sucked on one tight and hungry breast and she gave a sharp gasp of pleasure.

Her fingers faltered with the buckle of his belt as she felt him slide the thong right off, his hands lingering suggestively on her bottom, and sliding briefly against the cool flesh of her inner thighs, until she was left wearing nothing but a pair of emerald-green high-heels.

He threw his shirt off and stepped out of his trousers and underpants just as Kate bent over to unstrap her shoes.

His eyes darkened. 'On second thoughts, I want to see you nearly naked. Leave those on,' he instructed softly, pointing to the shoes, as he led her across to the bed.

Now this really *was* mistress-like, Kate thought, torn between anticipation and self-consciousness, as the cool linen of the duvet whispered against her back. Having your dark, beautiful lover tower over you in a foreign bedroom, with you wearing nothing but a pair of very sexy, green shoes.

'You look like my every fantasy come to life,' he whispered, his voice deepening.

'How?' she whispered back.

'Wicked. Abandoned. And...'

She heard his hesitation, was intrigued by it. 'And what?'

'Here,' he admitted. 'Now. On my bed after too long. Waiting for me to make love to you over and over again.'

She closed her eyes, so that he wouldn't read the regret there. *Making love*. It was nothing but a turn of phrase. What they were about to do was a lot more basic than that. 'Then don't keep me waiting too long,' she said shakily.

*Wait?* Why, he could barely contain himself enough not to thrust straight into her as soon as his hands began to explore her. But she was as ready and as turned on as he was and it was only moments before he was poised against her.

Provocatively she parted her legs for him and then engaged in intimate capture, teasing him, edging him against her enticingly until he was completely in her power, and she in his.

It all happened so quickly. Too quickly, she thought as regret was dissolved by wave after wave of gut-wrenching pleasure by an orgasm which exploded into instant life.

'Giovanni!' she sobbed.

There was a long silence afterwards while they struggled for breath, and it was a long moment later before he looked down into her face, his dark brows criss-crossing as he saw the tears which slid from beneath her closed eyes.

'Why are you crying?' he asked quietly.

Because this was the only place she could find happiness, locked in the embrace of a man motivated only by desire. Hopeless.

'Because it was beautiful,' she answered, and that was no lie.

He pushed a damp strand of hair from her cheek. 'The best,' he agreed softly. 'The very best.'

'Thank you.'

'Don't mention it,' he said gravely, and then smiled. 'You want to stay here, or do you want to go out and eat?'

'It's too late, surely?' she protested.

'They eat very late in Spain. Didn't you know?'

'I don't know if I can be bothered to get dressed.' She yawned, unwilling to leave this room, to shatter the curious air of intimacy which had somehow evolved between them.

'Then I can ring down for Room Service?'

'Mmm. That sounds better.'

She feasted her eyes on him as he walked naked across the room to the telephone, and heard him issue a number of requests in what sounded—to her untutored ears—like fluent Spanish.

When he turned around he saw her watching him, her eyes alive and on fire, and then saw her face close, as if she was keeping something secret from him. For a man brought up in a culture where secrecy was second nature, it was oddly disconcerting.

'You're happy?' he asked suddenly.

'Of course.' She drew in a deep breath and looked at him. She had to know. 'Did you...did you...see Anna?'

He turned away, but not before she had seen the dark look of regret which haunted his eyes, and it stabbed straight through her heart.

'Isn't this a rather strange time to ask me a question like that?' he returned in a harsh, cruel voice.

She had to know where she stood. She *had* to. 'Did you?' she persisted.

'Yes. Yes, of course I did.' There had been two tense, fraught meetings before Anna had realised that the clock could not be put back. He had told her sincerely that he wanted her to find happiness with someone who deserved her quiet devotion. She had told him to go to hell and somehow that had made him feel better.

'How is she?'

He turned back again. 'Do you really care?' he demanded.

'Of course I care! Do you think I feel good about what happened?'

'I feel a lot worse about it than you do, *cara*, let me assure you.' He gave a short laugh. 'The last I heard, she had cut her hair and was flying to stay with her sister in Rome, who is promising to give her the time of her life.'

Still, there was something else she needed to know. 'So there is no chance of a reconciliation?'

'Kate,' he said dangerously, 'if this was troubling you then should you not have asked me before you agreed to come out here?'

'I suppose so——'

'But you didn't?'

'No.' She bit her lip as she recognised the truth, that she had wanted to see him to the exclusion of all else—of pride...even of common decency.

He shook his head as if in quiet disbelief. 'Did you really imagine that I would betray her for a second time with you?'

'Is that all I am to you?' she said bitterly. 'A betrayal?'

In a sense, yes, she was, but she was more than that. His reaction to her had illuminated the fact that he did not have the steely control he had once thought defined his character. She was his weakness, too.

'Would you be here tonight if I thought that?' he grated.

'It might have been easier if you had found yourself a different bed-partner,' she said stiffly. 'Someone who didn't have such tainted associations as I clearly do.'

'But I didn't want another bed-partner. I wanted you.' His eyes were luminously blue as he came to sit on the edge of the bed, his finger ruefully tracing the tremble of her mouth. 'I wanted to see you again,' he said starkly. 'I had to see you again.'

But she thought that he made her sound like an addiction he couldn't wait to be rid of. 'Can I have a drink now, please?' she asked him as a diversion.

'You can have anything you want,' he smiled.

Except his heart.

'*Magara mia*,' he whispered.

'What's that?' she whispered back.

There was more regret in his face as he shrugged. 'My witch.'

But witches could work magic, and there was no spell she could put on Giovanni to make him love her as she loved him. Lucy had been right all along, Kate realised. Because from unconventional beginnings had grown a feeling which now consumed her.

He gave her a robe to wear, and put one on himself, and then opened champagne just as the food arrived—tiny little tapas which he laid out on a table overlooking the glittering city.

Kate forced herself to forget her useless longings, to enjoy the view and the food and the man who sat before her, enchanting her with little looks of longing as he fed her morsels of delicious food with his fingers.

# CHAPTER ELEVEN

KATE had rarely felt so nervous as she dressed for dinner the following evening—and her nerves were compounded when she emerged in her towelling robe from the shower to have Giovanni casually drop a large, flat beribboned box onto the still-rumpled bed.

'What's that?' she asked him.

His eyes glittered. 'Why not open it, and see?'

Beneath the layers of tissue paper lay the most beautiful lingerie she had ever seen—silver silk-satin and filigree lace. Bra. Camiknickers—and a wisp of a garter belt. Kate swallowed as she pulled each delicate item out of the box. 'It's…'

He heard the strained quality in her voice, and frowned. 'You don't like it?'

'How could I not like it?' she questioned shakily. 'It's utterly beautiful.'

But her reaction had not been the delight he had anticipated. 'Will you wear it tonight, *cara*?' he instructed silkily. 'For me?'

She slid the garments onto her still-damp skin, aware that his eyes were devouring every trembling movement she made. The silk felt unbelievably light and delicious as it clung fluidly to every curve, but she couldn't rid herself of an unreasonable sensation of disappointment.

Because as he himself had pointed out the fripperies were such a typical gift of a man to his mistress that she felt almost as if *she* was being stereotyped by the man who had once accused her of the same thing. And now she was being cast into a one-dimensional role from which there could be no escape.

126

She forced herself to smile as she turned slowly for her captive audience. 'How's that?'

A pulse beat deep within his groin, and he wished that he could cancel the dinner. 'Exquisite,' he murmured throatily. 'It seems a pity that you have to cover them up.'

'You mean that you'd like other men to see me like this?' she demanded wildly.

Jealousy—hot and dark and potent—flooded over his skin. 'They are for my eyes only,' he told her dangerously, but something in the reproachful tremble of her lips made him adjust his tone. 'Just the image of you wearing them will sustain me through dinner, and I will imagine myself removing them later,' he promised.

She wore one of her new dresses—a deceptively simple robe, cut on the bias, which skimmed the floor. Its plain, almost stark cream colour provided the perfect foil to the living fire of her hair, which she clipped back at the sides and let tumble to her waist.

He murmured his approval as she stood in front of him.

And Giovanni looked exquisite, too—in the beautifully cut black dinner suit and a snowy silk shirt. Formality suited him, she thought, but then, in a way, he was almost old-fashionedly formal in his outlook.

His behaviour towards her, as his mistress, was exemplary. He had flown her to a beautiful city and bought her fine underwear. He was the most skilled and considerate lover, and now he was taking her out to a fancy restaurant to meet business colleagues of his.

If only there could have been a little more *warmth* in his attitude towards her—but warmth implied emotion, didn't it, and there was precious little where he was concerned? Which made it imperative that she keep her own feelings hidden.

The restaurant was crowded and had the lively buzz of success about it. The others were already seated and

Giovanni introduced her to Xavier and Juan, and Juan's wife, Rosa.

Very Spanish, with their dark, flashing-eyed looks, Kate thought that both men were attractive, but Xavier especially so. His eyes narrowed appreciatively as she walked in at Giovanni's side, and he made a great play of bending to kiss her fingertips in an impossibly chivalrous manner.

'Giovanni did not tell me that *you* would be *quite* so beautiful,' he murmured in perfect English.

Giovanni took Kate's hand to his lips and let it linger there in an action which was decidedly possessive. 'And I did not tell Kate that *you* were quite so presumptuous! Be careful, *cara*—Xavier has quite a reputation with women!'

Kate laughed, enjoying his territorial display. 'I'll heed your warning,' she told him.

Rosa was not so forthcoming, and her polite smile at Kate was undoubtedly iced with frost, though Kate doubted whether any of the men had noticed.

They drank expensive wine and ordered food, and Rosa subjected her to a gentle little grilling, which to the outside world must have sounded like genuine interest. But the look in her brown eyes told a different story.

'You have known Giovanni long, Kate?' she asked quietly.

How to answer this? She had *known* him for about three and a half months, but the reality boiled down to about fifteen hot and steamy days. Kate turned her eyes desperately to Giovanni for assistance.

'We met at my godmother's house, back in July,' he said smoothly.

'Oh!' Rosa's plucked eyebrows shot upwards in two delicate arcs. 'You are a friend of Giovanni's godmother?'

Don't let her intimidate you, thought Kate. 'Our relationship is a working one,' she said staunchly.

'You *work* for her?' quizzed Rosa.

She was making her sound like Lady St John's *cleaner*,

thought Kate indignantly. 'In a sense. I decorate her homes for her.' She smiled, with an effort.

'*Oh!*' said Rosa again, and curved her lips into a smug, little smile.

The fish course was brought, and Kate felt as if she were ploughing through sawdust, but she finished most of it, washed down with the occasional mouthful of white Rioja.

Across the table, Giovanni watched her. Outwardly, she was completely at ease in the luxurious surroundings, and her table-manners were a delight to observe, and yet she seemed unaccountably *nervous*, and he wondered why.

Surely the sight of Xavier looking as though he would like to devour her for courses one, two, three and four was not making her look almost self-conscious—a quality he had never associated with Kate. He sent Xavier a searing look, and this was interpreted with a rueful shrug.

Before the dessert, Kate got up to use the powder room, and Rosa got to her feet at the same time.

'Let's go together,' she said prettily. 'And then the men can talk about us while we're away!'

'We'll be talking football, I can assure you,' said Giovanni mockingly.

In the powder room, all pretence slid away as Rosa turned to Kate, an undisguised look of hostility on her face.

'So,' she observed slowly, 'you are the woman responsible for the breaking up of Anna and Giovanni's engagement.'

The mention of Anna's name made Kate's cheeks flush hot and she thought that it must look like an admission of guilt. 'You know Anna, do you?'

'But of course.' Rosa shrugged. 'She and Giovanni were together for such a long time—'

'How long?' asked Kate, without thinking about the folly of asking such a question.

'You don't *know*?' The smile grew superior. 'No, I suppose you wouldn't. Well, my dear, they were together for eight years.'

Kate felt all the blood drain from her face and had to grip onto the handbasin to stop herself swaying. Eight years! That long!

'You *do* look guilty,' observed Rosa, her soft tone unable to disguise the barb in her voice. 'I expect that I would feel exactly the same—but then I can never imagine doing what you have done to another woman.'

Kate wanted to cry out and defend herself. To tell this woman that she had not known of Anna's existence. That Giovanni had not told her. But something stopped her—and she wasn't sure whether it was loyalty to Giovanni, or a sinking worry about whether she would have behaved differently even if she *had* known about Anna.

Instead, she fixed a bland smile onto her lips. 'I think we'd better get back now, don't you—or the men will wonder where we are?'

Somehow she got through the rest of the meal without letting her smile slip, aware that Giovanni was watching her closely.

And once they were back in the car he didn't start the engine, just turned to look at her. 'What is the matter with you?' he demanded. 'You've been acting strangely all evening!'

She wasn't going to blab. She pretended to search in her handbag for a tissue she didn't really want. 'Nothing.'

'Yes, there is something,' he contradicted. 'Look at me! Something was wrong tonight, Kate, and I demand to know what it is!'

She looked up and glared at him. 'You lay no claim on me! You cannot demand *anything* of me, Giovanni!' she told him proudly. 'Nothing!'

He almost smiled at her defiance, but he remained resolute. 'Was something said?'

Kate sighed, recognising a persistence and a determination about his character which was very similar to her own. Giovanni would push and push and push until she gave him the answers he required. Better, she supposed, to give in gracefully now, rather than ruin the rest of their last precious night together.

She stared out at the night. 'Rosa spoke of Anna—'

An abrasive word was torn from his lips. 'She had no right! It is not her business!' he snarled, and then his voice grew softer. 'What did she say?'

Kate shifted uncomfortably in her car-seat. 'It doesn't matter.'

'Kate,' he said, on a dark note of warning, and she stared unhappily into his glittering eyes. 'It matters.'

'I had no idea that you had been together for so *long*!' she said despairingly. 'Eight years! That somehow makes it all the worse!'

Her pain affected him more than it had any right to. 'It is the custom in Sicily,' he told her gently, 'for engagements to be long ones.' His face altered into a grim mask. 'I will speak to Rosa,' he said in a voice of deadly venom.

'No, Giovanni! You mustn't!'

'*Mustn't?*' he repeated imperiously, as if he had never been forbidden to do something by a woman in his life. 'Don't forget, you lay no claim on me either, Kate.'

'But what point is there in saying anything—it'll only cause trouble?' she asked him urgently. 'You've known Rosa and her husband for years and years—you can't fall out, just because of me!'

'Thank you for your consideration, Kate,' he said implacably. 'But I will say a few quiet words. Don't worry, *cara mia*,' he tilted her face upwards and coaxed a smile, 'we will not fall out.' He wasn't going to tell Kate that Rosa was probably jealous of her, and that the wife of one of his oldest associates had been giving him the come-on for the past year. Giovanni's mouth hardened. It was time he warned her off.

'Kate?'

'What?'

He bent his head forward and planted a soft kiss on her lips, smiling as he watched her eyes flutter helplessly to a close. 'Let's make the most of our last few hours in Barcelona,' he whispered urgently. And he wasn't talking sightseeing.

He drove as if demons were at his heels, and, back in the hotel room, he stripped her clothes from her body with such slow, sensuous care that she wanted to beg him to hurry up.

But the waiting and the anticipation more than compensated for her mounting need for him, and only when she was lying in the beautiful silver undergarments on the bed did he remove his own clothes and come to lie on top of her.

She saw the look of dark hunger on his face and gestured to the camiknickers she still wore, a question in her eyes.

'I want to leave them on,' he whispered. 'I want to do this.' And he pushed aside the panel which shielded the very core of her femininity, his finger coming away coated with the syrup of her longing and he groaned and positioned himself and thrust into her long and slow and deep.

The sensation of the silk still against her skin, and then the silk of him inside her skin was almost too much too bear, and frantically she clung to him as he kissed her, and rocked her with the oldest rhythm of all.

And then it was too late, it was happening all over again, and this time she had to concentrate very hard to keep her emotions in check.

Because this time she was determined not to cry.

Kate felt subdued as she stood close to the departure lounge, but she hoped that she achieved the right kind of grown-up expression. The kind of look which would tell him that she had enjoyed herself—though she guessed he must have known that. A look which would tell him she had no expectations about the future.

She wondered what he would say. Just a goodbye, and then a brief, poignant kiss, maybe?

Giovanni looked down into eyes as green as the cypress trees which dotted the hills around the place of his birth, and touched his mouth to hers.

'So did you enjoy your visit to Barcelona, Kate?' he murmured.

To be honest, they could have been in any city in the world, for all the sightseeing they had done, but then sightseeing hadn't been number one on their agenda. She knew that and he knew that.

She nodded, and smiled, her smile masking the thought that this might be the last time she would ever see him. 'You know I did.'

'Mmm. I thought so, *magara mia!*'

'I am *not* your witch!'

His eyes narrowed. 'Your Sicilian is improving by the day!'

Her flight announcement was called for the second time, and he swore softly beneath his breath. Had two days really passed with such indecent speed?

'Giovanni, I really *must* go—'

He halted her with a forefinger placed softly over her lips. 'Listen, I'm going to Roma in a few weeks' time. Would you like to come and join me there?'

Her heart leapt, even while she registered how casually he broached the question. She pretended to give the question careful consideration, determined not to seem too eager.

'To Rome?' she repeated, and then she smiled. 'Do you know, Giovanni?' she said, taking care to keep her voice as casual as his. 'I've always wanted to visit Rome.'

\* \* \*

Rome. Paris. Prague. Vienna. New York. She joined him in
one luxurious hotel after another—and in between times Kate
threw herself into her work in an attempt to consume her
thoughts with something other than her dark Sicilian lover.
But it wasn't easy.

Christmas came and went, but she didn't see him. He spent
it with his parents in Palermo, while Kate and Lucy went to
their own family home.

Giovanni sent her a package which she dared not put beneath her parents' Christmas tree, imagining more of the exquisite lacy undergarments he had made a habit of buying
for her—and she could just imagine what her father would
say about *that*.

But he surprised her with a Sicilian-English dictionary
with a mocking foreword written in his distinctive hand:
'Learn something new each day, *cara*—and then teach me
what you have learned.'

She devoured it during the holiday—oblivious to the
sounds of carols or the lure of mince-pies and turkey—mem-
orising as many words as she thought might be appropriate
to relate when next she saw him...and resolutely casting
aside the word 'love'.

'You're still crazy about him, aren't you?' asked Lucy one
morning in late January, when she and Kate had been going
through her expenses.

Kate had flown in from New York the evening before, still
glowing from Giovanni's lovemaking, a box of matching yel-
low lace underwear hidden away inside her suitcase.

'Not more?' she had asked him, her mouth curving into a
slow smile as she had taken another outrageous wisp of nothing from the box. 'You've bought me enough already,
surely?'

He had shaken his head as she began to pull the camiknickers up her long, long legs, knowing that very soon he
would be pulling them off her again. 'Never enough, *cara*,'

he told her huskily. 'You should have something different for every day of the year.'

And Kate found herself working out how many weekends she would have with him to enable him to be able to provide *that*.

She had taken a Thursday and Friday off work and had flown into Kennedy Airport on Thursday evening, to find Giovanni looking tense and strained, and she had teased him about it.

'You don't want me here?'

'I couldn't wait for you to arrive,' he admitted huskily and took her into his arms and kissed her with an urgency which thrilled her.

'Then why the long face?' she asked in the cab on the way to their hotel.

'Oh, some—' He said some vehement word in Sicilian. 'Some mix-up over a big consignment which was meant to arrive from Sicily last week, but didn't.'

She crossed one leg over the other, hearing him draw in an unsteady breath as he was treated to the briefest glimpse of lacy stocking-top beneath a creamy-white thigh. 'Shame,' she murmured.

And he laughed. What the hell did it matter—what did any of it matter—when he had her here, like this? 'A terrible shame,' he agreed gravely, as he reached for her in the darkened intimacy of the car.

They spent the next morning in bed and then travelled to Liberty Island, where the queues for the statue seemed to go on forever.

Giovanni's mouth tightened. 'Let's skip it for today,' he said roughly, thinking that all he wanted was to be alone with her again.

But Kate shook her head. 'Queuing will do you good,' she said firmly.

'Oh, really?'

'Yes. Really! We'll people-watch and then over dinner we can see if we agree or disagree.'

'On what?' he asked, mystified.

'Oh, who's brought their wife. Who's brought their mistress—that kind of thing!'

'Mistress is a very old-fashioned word,' he growled, inexplicably offended by the term.

She batted her eyelashes at him. 'It's a very old-fashioned occupation, darling—didn't you know?' But inside she was on a high. In these cities—foreign to both of them—she could be exactly what she wanted to be, and, more than anything else, she felt as if they were on equal terms.

That weekend—like all the others which had preceded it—passed all too quickly, and Giovanni seemed reluctant to let her go.

'I'm sick of departure lounges!' he declared vehemently, sliding his hands around her waist, and locking them possessively in the small of her back.

Well, so was she—but she was determined that his last memory of her would be a sunny smile.

'I'm not overfond of them, myself,' she whispered. 'But there you go! Now, Giovanni, that's the third and final call, so will you *please* let me go?'

He had complied, reluctantly, but stood watching her retreating back until long after she had disappeared from view.

'Aren't you?' asked Lucy.

'Mmm?' Lost in a dreamworld dominated by Giovanni and only Giovanni, Kate looked up at her sister absently. 'Aren't I what?'

'Crazy about him? Even more than before.'

There was a moment of silence. 'I guess I am.' How could she not be? 'He's gorgeous,' she sighed, then shrugged, as if it didn't really matter. 'Though I guess it's easy for him to be gorgeous—the situation is very beautiful, but very false.

We meet in glamorous destinations, we stay in glamorous hotels. We eat delicious meals and make delicious love, and then I come home again.' She looked at her sister candidly. 'I guess that's what it's like—being a mistress.'

'Yes,' said Lucy thoughtfully, 'I suppose it is. You're intimate in so many ways, and yet not intimate at all. You get the sex and the glamour—but none of the ordinary stuff that makes for companionship.'

Kate tried to make light of it. 'What, like washing his socks, you mean?'

'Something like that.' Lucy's green eyes were piercing. 'And he never says he loves you?'

'Never.'

'Nor express any desire for a bit more…permanence?'

'Never.' Kate saw the expression on her sister's face and sprang to his defence, as though her pride expected her to. 'He hasn't long come out of a broken relationship, remember? He's hardly going to want to leap straight back into another.'

'And you're happy for things to continue this way, are you, Kate—the long-term mistress?'

'Happy enough.' Because what was the alternative? Life without him was a million times worse than these snatched moments of bliss; she had already tried that.

'And what's he like, during these weekends?' persisted Lucy.

'Perfect,' answered Kate simply. 'Absolutely perfect.'

'Not mean or moody any more?'

'No.' Kate looked at her sister with an air of defiance. 'I may be besotted with the man, but I'm not into masochism, you know, Lucy. And what would be the point of spending time with him if he continued to be angry with me?'

That much, at least, had changed.

These days, they had almost as much conversation as sex, and Kate wanted that. She wanted shared experiences which she would be able to store up in her memory. She wanted to learn more about *him*.

And she had.

He had told her about his parents and his younger brother, and the house he had grown up in, in the hills outside Palermo. The brother was now ensconced in Rome, running that branch of the Calverri empire.

He described the beautiful villa he had bought for himself and Kate had wondered wistfully if she would ever see it. He had spoken about his early life, and the Sicilian culture, and its proud, aloof people, and Kate had nodded in comprehension, remembering the print-out from her computer.

For Giovanni epitomised the Sicilian man. Proud, yes. And aloof—yes, more than a little. He gave so much, but that was all. She knew as much of him as he would allow her to know, and yet at times she felt as though she knew him better than she knew herself.

But maybe that was because physically, at least, they were so perfectly in tune with one another.

He called the following week, when Kate was feeling out-of-sorts, even though she knew that she should be feeling delighted, because he had just suggested coming to London. But she had been feeling off-colour for days now, and was beginning to wonder whether she had eaten something which disagreed with her. Or whether it was a mild form of jet lag.

'London?' she questioned weakly as little spots danced before her eyes.

'That's right.' Giovanni frowned at the telephone. He had thought she would be pleased. 'What's the matter, Kate—have you grown too used to room service?' he teased. 'I don't have to stay at your place, you know, *cara*. We can always go to a nice hotel, and you can pretend to be a tourist in your own city!'

She took a deep breath and sank down onto the sofa, wondering why her legs felt as though they were made of cotton wool. 'No, that's fine—I'd love you to stay here. When are you arriving?'

He paused, his heart beating hard with excitement. He had things he needed to tell her. 'Tomorrow,' he told her.

A wave of nausea washed over her. 'Tomorrow?' she repeated feebly.

'This is not the rapturous response I expected,' he murmured drily. 'Don't tell me you're becoming bored with me, *cara*?'

Never! Not as long as there were planets edging around the skies! But Giovanni expected playful teasing, she knew that. Just as she knew how much the truth would send him spinning out of her orbit.

'I'll tell you when I see you,' she teased back.

'I can't wait.'

And normally, neither could she. Normally she would be counting the hours and then the minutes until he would be back in her arms again.

Only this time she did so for a different reason entirely.

Kate shivered as she heard his peremptory ring on the doorbell, and walked to answer it from the kitchen, where she had been making supper—even though eating was the very last thing she felt like doing.

She opened the door to him, as always unprepared for the glorious shock to her senses which his presence always seemed to invoke. But this time the sensation was all too fleeting. This time…

She bit her lip. 'Hello, Giovanni,' she said slowly. 'Come in.'

He frowned as he dropped his bags on the floor of the hall and shut the front door behind him.

'No kiss?' he accused softly.

'Let's go into the sitting room,' she said nervously. 'It's warmer in there.'

His eyes were watchful as he followed her. There was something different about her tonight. What was it? She seemed tense. Not herself at all. And pale, he thought—much paler than usual.

'Come to Giovanni, Kate,' he instructed softly.

How could she resist him? she wondered helplessly. How could she *ever* resist him? She went into the circle of his arms, raising her head so that he could kiss her.

Her body melted into his, and he felt the first heavy pulse of desire. 'That's better,' he purred when he eventually lifted his head. 'You seemed a little tense back there, *cara*.' He drifted the palm of his hand around the curve of her chin, a question in his eyes. 'What's the matter, Kate? Hmm? Busy week at work?'

Kate hoped that her bright smile did not look like a ghastly grimace. 'Er, yes. It *was* pretty hectic.'

'So now you relax. With me.'

Oh, God—she couldn't let him make love to her. Not now! Not yet! 'I've been preparing supper,' she told him wildly.

Supper? His obdurate expression hid his surprise. Usually food was remembered halfway through the evening as something of an afterthought. He surveyed her again, even though he went through the action of sniffing the air, in a parody of a hungry man returning home. 'I can tell,' he said indulgently. 'Smells good.' And then he frowned. More than smelling good, it smelt *familiar*. He frowned again. 'What is it, *cara*?'

She forced herself to inject some enthusiasm into her voice. After all, hadn't she spent hours preparing for what was supposed to be the surprise to end all surprises? Until…

'Can't you tell?' she asked him, her heart beating very fast with fear and foreboding.

He strode straight through into the kitchen, where it quickly became clear what she had done—the ingredients gave it away. He saw a pile of pasta and he peered at what lay within the simmering pot. Fresh sardines. And wild fennel. Currants and pine nuts and saffron. A slow smile dissolved his frown.

And very nearly dissolved her, too.

'*Pasta con le sarde*,' he murmured. 'Sicily's most typical dish. Oh, Kate, *cara mia* Kate—do you do this because you know that the way to a man's heart is through his stomach?'

Fear gripped her. If only he hadn't said that! As if she was trying to manipulate some kind of permanence with him. It was just a teasing, throwaway comment, but in view of the bombshell she was shortly to drop...

'Shall we eat?' she questioned hoarsely.

He told himself that she was nervous because she had obviously gone to a lot of trouble preparing this dish. He told himself that the timing was important—it could not be left to sit and spoil; its beauty was in its freshness and crispness.

But somewhere deep inside him there remained the disquiet that something was not quite as it should be.

She had laid the table carefully, as if her life depended on it. With napkins and candles and fresh flowers.

'This looks very welcoming,' he observed as she struck a match and lit the candles. 'The perfect supper.'

The last supper, she thought, with a sudden shiver of apprehension. 'Sit down, Giovanni,' she said huskily as she hovered in the kitchen doorway.

Almost imperceptibly he raised his brows. Was she *deliberately* staying far away from him physically, he wondered, or was he simply imagining it? 'Shall I open some wine?'

Not for me, she was about to say, until something made her bite the words back. 'That would be lovely,' she said weakly. 'And after that you could unpack, couldn't you— while I throw it all together?'

'Sure,' he said impassively, with an almost imperceptible elevation of his dark brows as he put the opened bottle of Sicilian red on the table to let it breathe.

He hung his clothes up, and placed a package for her on the bed and when he returned she was dishing the meal out. He sat down at the table and poured them both a glass of wine.

Kate sat down opposite him, glad for the relief thrown on their faces by the flickering candlelight. At least he wouldn't be able to read her expression.

He raised his glass to hers. '*Saluti!*' he said softly.

But she merely brushed her lips against the crimson liquid, she did not drink. Even the smell of it was making her stomach clench once more.

Giovanni ate his food, noticing that she did little but move hers around on the plate, arranging it in little piles, in order, he guessed, to appear as if she had actually eaten some of it.

He wondered whether she now saw the role of mistress as too submissive. His independent Kate. Had she decided that this kind of relationship was not for her? And how would he respond if she did? Would it be easy just to let her go?

He sighed and put his fork down, his news forgotten. 'Do you want to tell me about it?' he questioned.

She stared at him. 'Tell you about *what*?' she whispered hoarsely.

He noted her surprise, and its implication irritated him. 'You think I don't know you well enough to know when something is wrong, Kate?' he demanded. 'You think that all I notice is the way you are when I make love to you? That I am completely obtuse as a man?'

She shook her head. 'Giovanni…' She couldn't say it; she couldn't.

'*Matri di Diu!*' he swore as he saw the increased whitening of her face. 'What is it, Kate? Tell me!'

There were only words now. Bald, bare words—because nothing could disguise or cushion the unpalatable fact she was about to tell him.

'I'm pregnant,' she said flatly.

# CHAPTER TWELVE

FOR a moment, Giovanni's world imploded. He thought he heard the loud beating of a clock, but there was no clock in Kate's dining room, so it must have been the thundering of his heart.

He stared across the table at her. 'What did you just say?' he asked in a voice which was dangerously calm.

She had thought that she had seen his face in almost every guise. She had thought that she had seen his anger before, but the anger which darkened and hardened his features now was truly monumental. She tried to tell herself that he was shocked. Naturally, he was shocked.

She tried again. 'I'm pregnant.'

There was a loud crash and at first Kate thought that it was the sound of his chair being scraped back, and of Giovanni rising menacingly to his feet. But the crash had been the glass of wine he had knocked over. The glass had not broken, but the wine had spilt out and seeped all over the white damask table-cloth like a puddle of blood, and neither of them made a move to stop it.

His heart was pounding in his ears. 'It cannot be my baby,' he told her with cold emphasis. 'Can it?'

The indignity and the implication made her cheeks sting. 'Of course it's your baby!' she declared, and she trembled her way to her feet, facing him, her breath ragged, as if they were two combatants in a boxing ring. 'Whose could it be if not yours?'

'I have always made absolutely sure that you could not become pregnant,' he said, still in that cold, deadly voice. 'You know that!' He approached her round the table with all the dangerous stealth of a jungle cat, while a hot rage burned inside him. 'Has there been someone else, Kate? Some man who wasn't quite so careful while I was away? You are a highly sexed and very responsive woman, we both know that. Tell me the truth, Kate, and I promise not to judge you.'

*Judge* her? He might as well have torn her heart from her chest. There was a ringing smack as the flat of her hand connected with his cheek, but he did not flinch, merely raised his own hand in lightning-fast reaction to imprison her wrist and to haul her close to him. So close that she could feel his warm, angry breath—see the furious black glitter of his eyes.

'Whose is it?' he demanded.

'Yours! Yours! Yours! *Yours!*'

Her mouth taunted her victory at him. The oldest trick in the book. Damn her! Damn her! And his anger transmuted into something else—something which was about as earth-shattering as he could imagine. The realisation that something of him would now be carried on into the next generation. His own little piece of immortality. She was carrying his child! His!

'Mine?' he questioned, but now there was a wondering note to his voice. 'Mine, *cara*?'

'Yes.'

With a dazed look in his eyes, he lowered his mouth irresistibly down on hers and began to kiss her in a kiss which was very close to tender.

But the kiss went the way of all their kisses, and the tenderness—was it real or imagined? wondered Kate heatedly—swiftly became desire, pure and sharp and undiluted.

She told herself not to respond, to push him away as he deserved to be pushed after the hideous accusations he had made, but her body would not heed her. It was too finely tuned to his sensual mastery to be able to do anything other than to spring into instant and urgent life beneath his touch. This was the father of her child, she thought weakly—the man who had created this new life growing within her, who could create all life in her.

'Giovanni!' The word came out in an exultant little whisper as he kissed her with a fervour which surpassed his normal kisses. And it was easy to forget the cruel things he had said to her when he kissed her like that.

Her thready little moan excited him even more, and without warning it was suddenly about much more than kissing. He was beyond thought, beyond reason, pursuing some blessed communion with her.

'Giovanni,' Kate breathed in disbelief, because now his hands were rucking up her skirt, and his fingers were snapping at the delicate lace of her panties, so that they fell uselessly to the floor. And with his other hand he was unzipping himself. 'Giovanni!' she whimpered, but the word sounded more like a plea than a protest, and it was. God, help her— it *was*!

He found himself driven on by a life-force so primeval that he could barely think, barely hear—all he could do was feel…feel *her*. He looked down at her mockingly as his fingers flicked enticingly against her molten heat. 'You want me to stop, *cara*? I don't think you do, but tell me yes, and I will.'

'Yes! Yes! *Oh*, no!' she sobbed as he touched her again, oh, so intimately, and she squirmed with excitement. 'No, don't stop! Please, don't stop! Do it! Do it! Do it to me! Now!'

Her words incited him almost as much as the frantic movements of her hips and he pushed her against the wall and levered her legs up around his waist, gasping aloud as he entered her, thrusting into her again and again, losing himself in pursuit of that sweet destination.

This might be the very last time that the man she had grown to love might take pleasure in her arms, she realised.

Heartache ripped through her, but somehow he banished it with every insistent movement of his strong, virile body.

Briefly she opened her eyes to see what a decadent picture the pair of them made—his trousers at his ankles, her skirt pushed up to her waist. How could he ever respect a woman who let him do something like this? But then she began to dissolve in the familiar ecstasy, and her greedy body began to convulse about his. She heard his helpless moan as he spilled his seed into her, and then let his head fall against her shoulder, his lips against her neck.

Kate closed her eyes. What had she done? She had let him take her like that, after his sickening reaction to her momentous news. Had she no shame where this man was concerned? No pride?

She let her feet slide to the floor and pushed him away, tired now. And weary. Impossibly and hopelessly weary. She was aware of the irony of what had just happened. The first time that he had ever made love to her without using any protection. Though it was a little late in the day for protection now.

She stumbled from the dining room and collapsed on the sofa, praying that he would just go. Go away and leave her alone with her fate, and she need never see him again.

She didn't hear him come back into the room, the first time she became aware of his presence was when she found him standing in the doorway, studying her, his face shadowed. And grave. As if he had just received some very bad news, which, in a way, she supposed he had.

'Are you all right?' he questioned, but he made no move towards her.

All right? How could he ask her a question like that at a time like this? 'I'm fine,' she said, still with that flat, tired note in her voice. 'Under the circumstances.'

'Kate, we shouldn't have…' His voice tailed away, and it

was the first time Kate had ever seen him look remotely uncomfortable.

'Shouldn't have what, Giovanni?'

His eyes narrowed. 'Made love like that, of course!'

'That wasn't called making love,' she told him scornfully. 'That was having wham-bam sex up against the wall!'

His mouth hardened. 'Is that why you begged me to do it to you?'

Shuddering at the memory, Kate raked a hand to scoop the damp red hair which had fallen over her face. 'It's irrelevant now, anyway. It's happened.' It's over, she thought, with a certainty which ached at her heart.

'Yes.' He found himself staring down at her flat belly. 'How far gone are you?'

She stared up at him as she considered his reasons for asking this. 'I'm going to keep the baby!' she declared wildly. 'You can't stop me from having it!'

For a moment the import of her words remained unclear to him, and when he understood their true meaning he stared at her with a look of furious distaste. 'Do you really think I would try?' he asked.

Relief flooded through her, and she shook her head slowly. 'No,' she said. 'No, I don't.'

'Then why say it?' he demanded. 'To hurt me? To insult me?'

'We all say things under pressure,' she returned. 'You said a few pretty wounding things yourself.'

'Yes.' He narrowed his eyes as he looked at her, unexpectedly vulnerable in her new-found condition. 'Kate—'

'I want you to know that this isn't some kind of trap to get you to commit to me,' she interrupted proudly, before he had the chance to make the accusation himself. 'Unless you think I somehow punctured one of the condoms with my fingernails when you weren't looking!'

'Of course I wasn't suggesting that!' he exploded. 'I was

just…shocked…taken off-guard. I didn't know what I was saying.'

'We're both shocked. Naturally.'

He studied her pale features and wanted to take her into his arms and smooth away the troubled look on her face, but her body was stiff with tension. She did not want him near her, he acknowledged—and who could blame her? He forced out the unbelievable words. 'You still haven't told me how pregnant you are.'

There was a pause. 'Eight weeks.' She watched him doing sums in his head. 'It must have happened in Rome,' she added.

Giovanni nodded. Yes, Rome.

He remembered her arrival. She had not been nervous, as she had been initially during that first trip to Barcelona. She had been the independent and confident Kate of their very first meeting, and he had been swept away by her.

Her beauty had been almost incandescent—like a fiery light which had surrounded her, and he had bathed in it. So had he been careless? So eager to lose himself in her that he had neglected to protect himself properly?

Kate watched him. 'But it doesn't really matter where or when or how, does it?' she asked heavily. 'The fact remains that it happened. Is happening,' she emphasised painfully, and placed the palm of her hand on a still-flat stomach.

'Yes,' he said, for what else was there for him to say? That he was delighted? No. She would scent his hypocrisy immediately—she was far too perceptive to be given plati- tudes which disguised his true feelings.

Kate sucked in a breath as she saw his expression of dis- quiet. She must tell him that she was not planning to use this situation to imprison him in a life not of his choosing. Her gaze was very level as she looked at him. 'Listen, Giovanni. I want you to know that I'm going to go ahead with the pregnancy. I'm going to have the baby and bring it up myself.'

'And me?' he questioned savagely. 'You've got it all worked out, haven't you? Don't I feature in this whole scenario? Or are you planning to exclude me from this baby's life, Kate?'

She tried to play fair, even though her heart told her how difficult it would be to cope with the occasional paternal visit from him. 'You shall have as much or as little of this baby's life as you choose to have,' she said carefully.

'And that's what you want, is it?'

She didn't answer that, not straight away. Of course it wasn't what she wanted! What she wanted was the impossible—the happy little trio of a real family, with Giovanni the doting partner and the doting father at her side. But he hadn't offered that, had he? Nor shown any sign of wanting it—certainly not before her announcement today—and even if he offered it now she could not contemplate a life with Giovanni staying beside her simply because it was his *duty*.

'In the circumstances, there isn't a lot else I can do,' she answered quietly.

Her cheeks looked so translucent, as if her skin were made of rice-paper, and he felt his heart lurch as he realised how traumatic this all must have been for her. First of all finding out, and then having to tell him, fearing his wrath. And oh, he had given it, hadn't he? Attacked her and blamed her when, in reality, she was blameless. 'I'll make you some coffee.'

'I don't want any coffee—'

'You need something,' he insisted forcefully. 'You look terrible!'

She didn't have the energy or the inclination to make a joke about that, and if the truth were known she *felt* terrible. Sick and troubled—and weren't pregnant women supposed to feel glowing and radiant?

Maybe pregnant women whose futures did not look like some unknown black, gaping hole they were being forced to leap into.

He was in the middle of heaping coffee into the pot when he heard her strange, muffled cry, and the spoon fell unnoticed from his fingers—some terrible fear, some awful foreboding telling him that something here was very, very wrong.

He ran into the sitting room to find her doubled up, clutching at her abdomen, and rocking to and fro with tiny fraught cries coming from her lips.

'Kate!' He was by her side in an instant, and as she looked up at him he saw pain in her eyes. And terror. 'Kate!'

He crouched down to her level. 'What is it, *cara*?' he questioned with soft urgency. 'Is it the baby?'

'I'm…' Her fingers waved awkwardly to where she could feel the unmistakable warm flood of blood against her thighs. 'Giovanni—there's a pain! A bad pain!' She reached out and clutched onto his arms, because right at that moment he seemed like the only sure foundation in her disintegrating world. 'Help me, Giovanni,' she whispered. 'Please, help me.'

Her plea smote at his heart, and gently but swiftly he disengaged her fingers and went to the telephone, where he made a rapid call.

She lifted her head painfully. 'What are you doing?'

'Phoning the hospital.'

'I don't need to go to hospital—'

'Kate, yes, you *do*,' he denounced sternly. 'And, what is more, you *will* go!' He began speaking and gave the address, looking round at her as he did so, wishing that he could obliterate that look of agony etched all over her delicate features. He replaced the receiver. 'The ambulance is on its way. Do you want me to tell your sister?'

Through the mists of pain she hesitated. Sometimes she and Lucy felt more like twins than sisters. She nodded. 'Yes.'

'And does she know? About the baby?'

'What baby?' she cried hysterically. 'There isn't going to *be* a baby, is there? But no, I haven't told her.' She hadn't told anyone, as if by not doing that could make it not seem real.

Lucy arrived at the same time as the paramedics, who were carrying a stretcher. She took one wild look of disbelief at Kate lying huddled miserably on the sofa, with Giovanni stroking a cool cloth at her brow, and her mouth fell open in horror.

'What's happened?' she demanded, her eyes flying accusingly to Giovanni. 'What have you done to her?'

He flinched, but he stood up to face the venom on her face quite calmly. 'Your sister is pregnant,' he said quietly.

'You bastard,' hissed Lucy, so that only he could hear.

'Lucy!' called Kate weakly, and she looked up into her sister's face, her green eyes swimming with the unbearable reality of what was happening to her.

She was losing Giovanni's baby.

'Oh, Kate, darling! Darling! What is it?'

'I think I'm having a miscarriage,' whispered Kate brokenly, and saying the hateful word made the first tears come—they slid freely down her cheeks and she made no move to dry them.

'We'll lift you onto the stretcher,' said the paramedic.

She shook her head. 'No, I'll walk.'

'Kate, either you go on the stretcher or I will carry you out to the ambulance myself,' said Giovanni grimly. 'Which is it to be?'

She heard the implacable note in his voice, and allowed herself to be lifted on.

'And will your partner—' the paramedic looked at Kate, and then to Giovanni '—be coming in the ambulance with you?'

Kate stared up into the blue gleam of his eyes, unable to

read any emotion in that shuttered expression. She thought about how babies *should* be conceived. Planned. With love. And preferably within the confines of a happy marriage. Not as the result of a matter-of-fact affair during a passionate weekend when contraception had somehow failed.

Giovanni did not want to be a father, nor her to be a mother. He certainly did not want her to carry *his* baby—so why subject him to the indignity of seeing this brief, precious life come to a premature end? Why should he be witness to a heartbreak he would be unable to understand?

'No,' she said huskily. 'I want my sister with me.'

He flinched again at the ultimate rejection. 'Very well, Kate,' he said flatly. 'I will wait here.'

He kept a vigil, only just preventing himself from ignoring her request and tearing down to the hospital to sit there and wait, and to interrogate the doctors and the nurses until he had news that she was safe and out of danger.

But Kate had expressly said that she did not want him to accompany her, and he came from a culture which treated a pregnant woman as a jewel above all others.

Except, as he reminded himself bitterly, that the chances were that she was no longer a pregnant woman.

Resisting the urge to smash something, Giovanni sucked in a hot, dry breath of pain. She was losing his baby, he thought, unprepared for the wave of despair which rocked him.

He kept himself busy by clearing away the remains of their meal. He winced as he imagined her making his country's most famous dish. Imagined her shopping for all the ingredients, knowing all the while what she had to tell him.

And what an unforgivable bastard of a man he had been.

He lifted the wine-stained tablecloth from the table and put it in the laundry basket, and settled down to wait.

He waited all night and well into the next morning.

He rang the hospital to be told that she had been 'taken to Theatre' and that her condition was 'stable'. He had wanted to shout down the phone at that point, to ask what on earth such a bland word could possibly mean when applied to a woman who had had a new life torn from her body.

He assumed.

He allowed himself a brief fantasy. That her pain and the blood—for he had seen the hideous blush of crimson for himself—had all been some kind of false alarm. Nature's way of warning her to take things easy. Perhaps the pregnancy was still viable.

But, in his heart, he feared the worst.

They would tell him nothing more. He was not a relative. She had not named him as her next-of-kin—that honour had gone to her sister. In the bureaucratic world of hospitals, he did not have a role in Kate's life.

She came home the following morning at eleven, accompanied by an even whiter-faced Lucy. The facts were stark and were spelt out to him by Lucy in the kitchen, whilst Kate slept fitfully.

There had been a baby, yes, but no more. The 'spontaneous miscarriage'—more hospital jargon, he thought grimly—had been followed by a routine operation to remove all traces of the pregnancy from her womb.

'*Routine?*' he questioned incredulously.

'That's what they said,' answered Lucy.

He saw how much she disliked him, and perhaps in a way he could not blame her, but, whatever the hospital thought and whatever Lucy thought, he *did* have a role in Kate's life. If no longer as her lover, then certainly as the man responsible for bringing her to this.

'I'll look after her now,' said Lucy fiercely.

He shook his head. 'No.' His voice was implacable. 'I will stay with Kate until she recovers.'

In the bedroom, Kate stirred and his words penetrated her

consciousness. *Until she recovers.* Then she heard Lucy speaking.

'You think it's that easy for her?' Lucy was saying. 'To recover from something like this?'

Kate pulled the duvet over her head to blot out the sounds of their voices. She felt weak and bereft as it was; she couldn't even begin to contemplate that Giovanni was planning to leave her.

Giovanni looked at Lucy. 'I will not share my thoughts with you, Lucy—they are for Kate's ears and Kate's ears alone.'

'And you really think that she *wants* you here?'

He looked deep into her eyes. 'Has she told you she doesn't?'

'How long will you be staying?'

He noted that she hadn't answered his question. 'Until her physical strength is such that she can fly,' he said quietly.

Her sarcasm showed on her face. 'What? Fly away from you?'

'To Sicily,' he said in a voice which brooked no argument. 'I intend taking her there to recuperate.'

Lucy stared at him. 'Are you completely out of your mind?'

He was tempted to tell her that it was none of her business, but—of course—it was. Kate was her sister and she was simply being protective.

'I appreciate your concern,' he said softly. 'But I do not intend to discuss it with you, Lucy.'

'I have never met a more stubborn man!' she exclaimed, shaking her head in frustration. 'Well, I'd better go. Please tell Kate I'm here whenever she needs me.'

'I'll tell her.'

After Lucy had gone, Giovanni went into the bedroom and stood looking down at her, and his face darkened as he saw her white features and shadowed eyes. He had done this to her!

Her eyes fluttered open as if she had sensed he was there. For a split-second she forgot why she was in bed at noon, with Giovanni observing her with such a tense, tight face, and then she remembered. 'Oh,' she cried, and she felt the hot well of tears behind her eyes.

He wanted to reach out to her, but she looked like a hunted animal, and so he sat on the edge of the bed instead.

'Kate,' he said softly, 'we have to talk about it.'

'Not now,' she said, and shut her eyes again, keeping them tightly closed, in a vain attempt to stop the tears streaming out.

# CHAPTER THIRTEEN

KATE woke early the following morning, with the warmth of sunshine piercing her senses, and the dull ache inside where her baby had been. She bit back the sob which had clawed at the back of her throat, and turned to stare at the wall.

'Kate?'

The smell of coffee wafted into the room and drifted towards her nostrils, and Kate turned over to see Giovanni standing in the doorway, a tray of coffee in his hands.

'Hello,' he said, but his voice was as sombre as his face.

'Hello.' She sat up in bed, forcing a smile.

'Here.' He put the coffee down on the dressing table and plumped up the pillows behind her back, and she settled against them comfortably.

'Thank you.'

He wondered what she was thanking him for, when he…he… A muscle moved at his mouth as he poured two cups of coffee and took one over to the bed and gave it to her. He let her drink some and saw a corresponding colour creep into her cheeks before he spoke.

'Kate, there is something I have to say to you.'

Through her mind shot a catalogue of statements she might expect now. Kate, it's over. Kate, it's been wonderful. Kate, Kate, Kate…

'Kate.' He saw her give a ghostly glimmer of a smile and wondered why. 'The miscarriage—'

'Please, don't!' she winced on a whisper.

'I caused it,' he said flatly. 'It was my fault.'

She stared at him with bewildered eyes and put the cup

156

down before she dropped the scalding remains of her coffee.
'*What?*'

'When I made love to you.'

'What are you talking about?'

'Do you think….?' For the first time in his life he was
having difficulty forming a sentence. 'Do you think the fact
that the…the…sex we had was quite—?'

Her pain made her want to hurt him, too. 'Quite what,
Giovanni?'

'Quite forceful? Do you think that was what caused the
miscarriage? *I need to know!*'

She stared candidly into his blue eyes, knowing that he
was seeking absolution and knowing that she would have
given it, had it been within her power. But it was not, and
her own guilt overwhelmed her. 'I don't know,' she said
honestly, and he buried his face in his hands.

'*Matri di Diu!*' he muttered hoarsely. 'What have I done?'

Part of her wanted to reach out and comfort him, but how
could she when she was so badly in need of comfort herself?
She closed her eyes wearily and lay back against the pillows.

They stayed there in silence for a little time, and then
Giovanni stood up.

'I'll make you breakfast—'

'I don't want any—'

'Oh, yes,' he said grimly, 'you do. Or rather your body
does. You will grow no paler than you already are, Kate, and
you will eat it if I have to mash it with a fork and feed you
like a baby. Is that understood?'

And, whilst the normal Kate might have rebelled against
such high-handedness, this frightened and hurting Kate was
glad to have him there, making her decisions and helping
make her well again.

She ate breakfast, then soaked in the bath that he had run
for her, and forced herself to dress—or, rather, she compro-
mised at dressing. A long, silky caftan which Lucy had

bought her for her twenty-first birthday, and the familiar light, loose garment was a little like wrapping herself in a security blanket.

When she walked into the sitting room Giovanni was sitting there and he stood up.

'Come and sit down. What can I get you?'

She shook her head. 'Nothing. You don't have to keep fussing over me, Giovanni.'

'I want to.'

She remembered his words to Lucy. He would stay until she recovered—so presumably he wanted her recovered in the shortest time possible.

He noted her silence, her normally mobile face grown inert, as if the life had been sucked out of it. And it had, he thought with a sudden fierce pain. It had. 'I want to take you back to Sicily with me,' he said suddenly.

How she had once longed to hear him say that! In her wildest fantasies she had imagined her clinging onto his arm, Giovanni's girl, the woman he had finally professed love to. 'You can't do that,' she said tiredly.

'Why not? You need to rest. You need the sun to warm your skin.'

She stared at him as though he was crazy. 'What about your family?'

'What about them?'

'What will they think of you bringing an English girl to their home—?'

'I have my own villa,' he interrupted gently, and, when he saw the expression on her face, added, 'with my own live-in housekeeper, so your reputation will not be tarnished.'

'Do they know about the baby?'

He shook his head. 'How can they, when I only found out myself the day before yesterday?'

'And what about Anna? Won't she want to come and find me and tell me exactly what she thinks of me?'

His shoulders tensed, the news which had seemed so important now totally insignificant in the light of what had happened. 'Anna is still in Roma.'

But would his family hate her? See her as the reason why his relationship with Anna had come to an end?

'Kate,' he said, in the gentlest voice she had ever heard him use, 'my family do not interfere. They know that I am a man, and expect me to make my own judgements about my life. They will respect you as my guest.'

'I don't know,' she said weakly.

'Well, I do. I am taking you to Sicily. I will look after you.'

Until she recovered. And then?

But she had no energy left to fight him. Nor any inclination, if the truth was known—and in a way it was rather a relief to let him take over everything. She did not see herself as passive, merely weary—and he seemed to have strength enough for the two of them.

And Kate knew that her willingness to go with him was about more than Giovanni's tenacity. She needed someone to look after her—but Lucy's partner was back—and as he was so often away, how could she ask Lucy?

She certainly couldn't go to her parents without explaining the circumstances, and she wasn't prepared to put them through that kind of hurt and disappointment. And, although the doctors had said she could start working as soon as she felt like it, the fact was that she felt completely empty inside. As though she had been blasted clean of all feelings bar one—that, no matter how useless she knew it to be, her feelings for Giovanni still burned as strong as ever.

'Well?' The blue eyes blazed into her.

'OK,' she nodded, and drifted back into a fitful sleep.

He stood and watched her for a time, until her breathing grew more even and her strained expression had relaxed with the onset of deep sleep. And only then did he lean over her to plant the lightest of kisses on her forehead. Then he moved silently from the room, his face dark with loss and pain.

Giovanni hired a plane the following day. He would not countenance the thought of the noise and bustle of airports, with Kate having to change planes and wait for connections. She was still pale, he noted with a pang—and quieter than he had ever known her.

She forced a smile. 'I'd better pack—'

'No, *I'll* pack some clothes for you,' he said.

'I'm not an invalid,' she protested.

Her wan little face made mockery of her words, and his heart clenched. 'I know that,' he agreed quietly. 'But I intend to look after you, Kate.'

It was ironic that the things she had always wanted to hear him say were now hers for the taking. Until she remembered that he didn't mean them—not long-term, anyway. He was falling into a role which he seemed to suit very well—that of macho protector. But it was only a temporary role, and one which he would relinquish once he was satisfied that she had recovered from her ordeal.

They flew out from the grey of a wintry English day and arrived to the warm, sensual air of a Sicilian spring. Kate hadn't known what to expect, and as the plane came in to land she could see hills awash with green—greener than she could ever have imagined.

He saw the surprise in her eyes. 'It is springtime,' he explained softly as the plane kissed the runway. 'And the very best, most beautiful time of all. You should see it in the summer when it gets diabolically hot, and the land becomes parched and brown and the harsh, unremitting wind they call the sirocco blows all around. Then Sicilians hide themselves indoors and away from the sun as much as they can.'

He had a car waiting, which he drove himself after carefully settling her into the back seat, a light cashmere rug tucked around her knees.

'But—'

'I know. You're not an invalid. Just enjoy it, won't you, Kate?' he added in what came pretty close to a plea—and how could she ever resist that?

The car began to mount the hills outside Palermo, where wild flowers of every imaginable hue studded the green hills. It was as pretty as anything she had ever seen, and Kate felt a great tug of something like longing. The land of his birth, she thought, and bit her trembling lip.

Towards the very top of the hill the car passed through wrought-iron electronic gates which slid silently open and closed behind them, just as silently and a beautiful long, low villa awaited them.

They were greeted at the villa by an elderly woman, dressed in a plain black dress, her face openly curious as she opened the door to them.

'This is Michelina, Kate.' He switched rapidly to Sicilian, and the woman inclined her head at Kate as Giovanni introduced them.

'Michelina has worked for my family in some capacity for many years,' he explained as he showed her along a shady passageway and into a luxurious marble-floored bedroom. Its windows were shuttered against the light of the day, and a large bed covered with an exquisitely embroidered cover loomed large in her vision. She turned to look at him with a silent question in her eyes, knowing that here lay another potentially painful moment of truth.

'This is where you will sleep,' he said abruptly, wondering if she was trying to test his resolve with that dewy-eyed look at him.

He felt the quickening of his heart. Was she trying to break him? To see whether he would repeat his outrageous behaviour of that terrible night when he had made such passionate love to her? Trying to break a man driven solely by his baser instincts, who could not nurture the woman who carried his child within her?

'And you?' she questioned, because she needed to know.

His mouth hardened. 'I will be along the corridor.'

So that was that. Looking after her would not include holding her in the night, and she must force herself to recognise—and to *accept*—that that side of their lives had come to a natural end. Perhaps it was for the best—at least this way she would be able to wean herself off him slowly.

Kate dressed for dinner that evening, wondering if she could bear it, and questioning her own sanity. For how could she possibly make a complete recovery if inside her heart was breaking?

But Michelina's presence meant that outwardly, at least, she was forced to behave as the perfect guest, and it quickly became tolerable for her to actually *feel* that way. She praised the wonderful food—though it was rather ironic that the housekeeper had chosen to present her with *pasta con le sarde* for her first evening.

'It is our national dish,' she told Kate with a smile, in her faltering English.

And Giovanni had glimmered a look across the table at her. 'Kate has heard of it,' he smiled.

'It's delicious,' she said, and it was. She had eaten barely anything of her own attempt at making the dish. She resolutely pushed that particular thought away, since looking back would not help her.

'You have many gastronomic feasts in store for you, Kate,' murmured Giovanni as he poured her a glass of wine. 'Sicilian food comes hotter, spicier and sweeter than the rest of Italy.' He gave a rueful smile. 'For which we must thank our Arab conquerors.'

She was yawning over the coffee Michelina had left them, when Giovanni stood up with an air of determination.

'You need to go to sleep now,' he instructed softly. 'Come with me.'

Outside her door, she wanted him to touch her—not in a sexual way, but in a comforting kind of way, to enfold her in his strong embrace and take some of the aching away, but he kept his distance.

Their physical closeness seemed like a distant dream as he quietly shut the bedroom door behind him, and she heard him moving off down the corridor.

But the sun was shining the next day and he drove her through the mountains to a resort along the Tyrrhenian coast called Cefalú, which he promised her was spectacular, and from the moment she saw the fishing village, squeezed between a long, curving sweep of sand and a massive peak known as the Rocca, Kate fell in love with it.

Giovanni slowed the car down, and pointed to the Rocca. 'What does that resemble?'

It was like one of those games you played with ink-spots, trying to make sense out of a random shape. Except that this shape seemed very clear to Kate.

'It looks like a head?' she guessed.

He laughed in delight. 'Clever girl! That's exactly what the ancient Greeks who came here thought, too. And kephalos is the Greek word for ''head''—hence Cefalú.'

Kate sat back in her seat, pleased at her perception and even more pleased by his smiling praise. At times like this, it was easy to forget her reason for being here—and easy to imagine that they were just like any other couple, enjoying the sights and relaxing in each other's company.

But they weren't, she reminded herself. They weren't.

She turned her head quickly to look out of the window. Too often in the past had she wished for the impossible and now it was time to change the game-plan.

Side by side, they walked down to the Norman cathedral and Giovanni gave her his linen jacket to wear.

'Women must cover their arms in this holy place,' he told her gravely as they stepped inside its cool, dim interior.

She felt as though she was being swept up into Sicily's stormy past as they walked around the majestic building in silence, and she studied her guidebook avidly. She insisted on lighting a candle, but her lips began to tremble as she did so, and her face was very pale when they re-entered the warm spring sunshine.

His eyes were assessing as he looked at her, but now was not the time nor the place for analysis. 'Lunch, I think,' he said firmly.

They found a restaurant whose sheltered terrace over-looked the fishermen's beach, and Giovanni ordered sword-fish for them both. And, when the waiter had left them with their water and basket of bread, he turned his gaze intently on her.

'Kate, we have to talk about it,' he said gently.

She wilfully misunderstood him, because surely it was too painful to contemplate the truth. 'The cathedral?'

'The baby.'

She shook her head, and her red hair flailed wildly around her shoulders. 'Who *says* we do? It was nothing, was it? An accident which happened, which mercifully—'

'*No!*' His negation was low, but savage—and his face burned with the intensity of conflicting emotions. 'Don't say that!' he grated. 'Don't you ever say that!'

'But it's the truth, isn't it? And for you it must have been...' she bit the words out painfully '...a relief.'

He shook his head and his words were quiet, almost bleak. 'How could something so negative ever be described in a positive way?'

She swallowed. 'Because we *didn't plan it*!'

'Out of all babies born, how many do you think are planned, Kate?'

Did she imagine the sadness in his voice, or did she simply

want to hear it there, to wish that he had wanted that baby just as much as she had? 'That's different, and you know it!' she responded fiercely. 'You didn't want a baby, Giovanni—so don't for heaven's sake now start saying that you did!'

He pondered her accusation in silence for a moment, knowing that she spoke the truth. 'And for you, Kate? Was it a relief for you, too?'

His gaze was so intense—as blue as the sea beneath them, and she could not insult him, or herself, by pretending that it had been nothing.

'Women feel differently about these things,' she told him haltingly. 'They may not have planned a baby, nor wanted a baby—but, once that baby is there, something primitive takes over—something outside all their control. Something that defies all logic!'

'Tell me,' he prompted softly.

'It's a protective thing, I guess. Nature's way of ensuring the survival of the species. A woman feels proud, and...sort of...*special*, when she knows she's carrying a child.' Especially the child of the man she loved.

'Well, you weren't acting proud and special the night you told me about it,' he observed.

'Oh, for heaven's sake, Giovanni!' She stared at him across the table. 'What did you expect? I anticipated your reaction...' She saw the look of remorse which darkened his features and she knew she could not bear him to feel she was attacking him. 'I *understood* your reaction,' she told him softly. 'The pregnancy came out of the blue. We had made no plans to commit—on the contrary, in fact—and it must have looked like the oldest trick in the book, from your point of view.'

He acknowledged her generosity and her understanding, even though he felt he did not deserve it, and knew then that he owed her nothing less than the truth himself. 'That's exactly what I felt at the time,' he admitted.

'I know. That's human nature,' she murmured. But oddly, now that it was out in the open, his admission had lost something of its sting.

His mouth hardened and he stared angrily down at the boats which bobbed on the water. 'And is it human nature to make love to a woman so violently—?'

'No!' she corrected, so fervently that he turned his head to stare deep into her emerald eyes, seeing forgiveness there. 'Not violently, Giovanni—*passionately*, and yes, there *is* a difference.'

'I shouldn't have done it!' He shook his head as he remembered the fever which had devoured him, a fever more intense than anything he had ever experienced.

'*You* didn't do anything, or, rather, you did—but I did it, too. I wanted you just as much as you wanted me. It felt...' She struggled to put it into words that would not make him feel trapped still, only this time by the strength of her unrequited feelings for him, rather than an unwanted baby. 'It felt primeval,' she said slowly. 'As though it had to happen, as if something had *compelled* it to happen.'

'Snap,' he murmured, and then his face darkened again as reality made its presence known. 'Except that our passion lost us the baby, Kate, didn't it?'

She wanted to take the hurting from him—because when he was hurting she was hurting, too. 'You can't know that!'

'I won't ever know, will I?' he questioned darkly.

But then the waiter arrived with their food and half a bottle of white wine, and as if by an unspoken mutual agreement the subject was suspended while they each tried to lose themselves in the beauty of their surroundings and the taste of the fresh fish.

She was sleepy after lunch, and he insisted on taking her back to the villa.

'Don't you want to sightsee some more?' She yawned.

He smiled. 'You forget—I know the island like I know my own face. These trips are for *you, cara mia.*'

Telling herself that it was merely habit now that made him call her that, she opened her mouth to object. 'But—'

'No buts, Kate. Now you take a siesta,' he ordered.

She couldn't have resisted that tone of voice even if she had wanted to. It seemed deliciously decadent to be going to bed in the middle of the afternoon, but it was not decadent at all, because Giovanni gave her a brief, terse goodbye, and left her at the door of her room once more.

The shutters were drawn and the room was a cool haven, but her heart was heavy as she sank down onto the bed. It wouldn't have killed him to hold her in his arms, surely? To give her the physical comfort and reassurance she badly needed right now.

But no, Giovanni was no hypocrite. He recognised that she was in a weakened state. He would not wish to be cruel to her by raising her hopes, only to dash them again. She must be strong, for the sake of her pride and her sanity.

And then the embrace of sleep claimed her, and she went willingly into its arms.

# CHAPTER FOURTEEN

THE midday sun streamed gold into the airy interior of the sitting room, and Giovanni lounged on the sofa as he waited for Kate to finish dressing for lunch. He gave a small groan as he shifted his position. Wanting her never got any easier, he thought. His body seemed to be in a permanent state of arousal.

They had spent the morning in Palermo, and he had taken Kate to the Calverri offices. His secretary had been polite—just—but he could see the naked curiosity in her eyes, wondering what this red-haired Englishwoman meant to her boss.

And now would come her baptism of fire, for within the hour—he glanced at his watch—his parents and his two aunts would be arriving for lunch. They had expressed a wish to meet her, and Kate had reluctantly agreed.

'But why do they want to?' she had asked.

'Kate,' he had replied patiently, 'you've been here for almost two weeks and they're rather curious about you, that's all.'

*That's all.* She had nodded. 'Oh, I see.'

'And I've never brought a woman to Sicily before.'

Well, of course he hadn't—there had never been any need to. He had had Anna—the fiancée whose name was never mentioned—the fiancée she secretly feared he was gearing up to go back to, which would account for his attitude towards her since they had arrived.

Oh, his behaviour had been impeccable—almost *too* impeccable. How aloof he had sometimes seemed as he had kept a courteous but definite distance.

Or maybe the miscarriage had killed all his desire for her.

Why else would he have gone so far out of his way to avoid any kind of physical contact with her?

'I bet your parents won't like me,' she moaned.

'Rubbish! Of course they will.'

But to Kate his voice sounded forced.

'And how will I speak to them? I only know about fifty words in Sicilian!'

'That's because I have taught you a new word every day,' he murmured. 'It seems we must increase your lessons, *cara*.'

Please don't flirt with me, her eyes told him silently.

He acknowledged the reproach with a narrowing of his eyes. 'And, besides, they speak perfectly good English—all my family do.'

'OK,' she had sighed. 'You win!'

But there was no taste of victory in his mouth, and he still had something he needed to tell her.

He looked up as she walked into the room, her bright hair newly washed and gleaming, a soft-green dress he had never seen before making the most of her tall, slim figure and those heart-stopping legs. Her skin was glowing with a light tan and the good food had filled out her hollow cheeks a little. She looked good enough to eat and, God, how he wanted her!

He couldn't seem to tear his eyes away from her, which wasn't doing his heart-rate any good whatsoever. 'You look…*spectacular, cara*,' he said carefully.

Well, make the most of it, she thought, hoping that her eyes held no trace of her unhappiness. Because soon she would be gone from here and gone from Giovanni's life for good.

'Thank you,' she said calmly.

'Come and sit down.' He patted the space beside him, then wished he hadn't, as she perched beside him, sliding her knees decorously together. 'Can I get you anything?'

She shook her head. 'No, I'm fine.' Which she supposed

she was. Well, physically, at any rate. The rest and the re-
cuperation had made her feel whole again. The warm sunshine and the good food had worked their simple magic, as
had the island itself, which Giovanni had shown her with the
loving pride of the true Sicilian.

It had been all too easy to suspend disbelief. To imagine
that this could go on and on—her and Giovanni, a happy
couple, to all intents and purposes.

Because once she had resigned herself to the fact that he
didn't want to share her bed any more it had—perversely—
allowed her to relax. Sex had always dominated their time
together, and it had only been here that true companionship
had entered the arena.

That didn't stop her wanting him, of course—she doubted
whether anything could ever put a stop to that, but at least
the absence of him in her bed was preparing her for a life
without him when she returned to England.

'What time are your family getting here?'

'In about an hour.' He paused. 'Kate, there's something I
need to tell you before they arrive.'

She looked up quickly, something in his voice warning her
that he wasn't about to start discussing what was on the lunch
menu. 'Oh?'

'It's about Anna.'

Her heart deafened her with a sickening thunder. 'I rather
thought it might be.'

He stared at her. Was she reading his mind now? 'You
did?'

Say it first, she urged herself. That way you emerge with
your pride and your dignity intact. Force yourself to con-
gratulate him and then he might remember you with at least
a modicum of respect.

'You're getting back with her,' she stated dully.

'*What?*'

'She's going to marry and become Mrs Calverri...'

There was a moment of stunned silence, and then he laughed. 'Yes. Yes, she is.'

How bloody insensitive could a man be? The smile she had intended feeling more like a grimace, she said stiffly, 'I hope you'll both be very happy.'

The laughter stopped. 'Do you, Kate?' he asked softly. 'Do you really?'

She was fast discovering that she wasn't *that* good a liar. She shifted right up to the other end of the sofa and glared at him. 'What do *you* think?' she demanded. 'Do you think I have no feelings?'

'You keep your feelings very well-hidden,' he commented.

'That's pretty rich—coming from you!'

'I am a Sicilian,' he drawled arrogantly. 'What's your excuse?'

'Well, you must be a grandmaster at concealment—if you've been playing the perfect host to me, whilst all the while…all the while…you…you…' Her words petered out; they had to—much more of this and she would be bursting into howling sobs of hurt.

'Kate—'

She shook her head. 'Perhaps I deserve it! After all, it's no worse than what I did to her—'

'No, what *I* did to her,' he corrected fiercely. 'It was my relationship and my responsibility. You were right, you know, Kate—you knew nothing of her existence. I should not have blamed you for my own weakness.'

There it was again, that hateful word. *Weakness*. Well, she would show him just how strong she could be! Fighting on every reserve she possessed, she pulled herself together with a steadying breath. 'I don't know if I can face having lunch with your parents—won't they see this as a conflict of interests? And what about Anna? Won't she be furious?'

'I doubt it,' he said slowly.

She stared at him in disbelief. 'What, her future in-laws fraternising with your secret lover?'

He frowned over the phrase and then his mouth twisted contemptuously. 'Never describe yourself like that again!'

'Well, I am, aren't I?'

This had gone far enough. He wanted to reach out and take her hand, but her arms were crossed so firmly across her chest that he didn't even try. 'Kate, Anna is getting married to my brother.'

She froze. Stared at him, wild hope being squashed by all-consuming insecurity. 'Say that again.'

'Anna is getting married to my brother.'

'Your *brother*?'

He heard the incredulity in her voice and understood perfectly—because his own reaction had been very similar. 'He's been working in Roma. Remember, I told you? Anna met him there, and...' He shrugged, a rueful smile playing about his lips. 'It now emerges that Guido is the man for her, that she is happier with Guido than she has ever been in her whole life,' he finished drily.

Wild hope—which had briefly triumphed—now lost out to insecurity. Just because he wasn't getting back with Anna didn't mean he wanted *her*, did it? You had only to look at his behaviour to know that he didn't.

'When did you find out?' she asked quietly.

His gaze was very steady. 'The night I arrived in London, the night...' His words tailed off. He had been feeling like a man free of chains that night. Anna's new-found happiness had given him a heady sense of freedom that he had been longing to convey to Kate. And new and very different chains had locked themselves around his heart.

'And was your pride wounded?' she asked flippantly, because a flip remark seemed the only way that she could push the memory of that night away.

He raised his eyebrows at her defiant pout, and the ache

intensified. He contemplated punishing her with a hard, sweet kiss, but at that moment there was a loud ringing at the front door.

'Saved by the bell,' he murmured resignedly.

Kate stood up hastily, smoothing down imaginary creases in her dress with hands which were suddenly clammy and she didn't know if that was a reaction to what he had just told her or apprehension about meeting a group of people she was still convinced would dislike her.

But in that she was wrong. True, his mother scrutinised her intently when they first shook hands, as did his two aunts. His father took one look at her and murmured something softly in Sicilian to his son, who gave a small smile in response.

Kate was seated between Giovanni's father, and his father's sister—an absolute delight of a woman named Maria. Giovanni had told her that she was his favourite aunt and she had a very dry sense of humour. And a way of asking questions which really made you want to answer them, though some questions were just too difficult to answer…

They ate *pasta alla Norma*—eastern Sicily's favourite pasta and supposedly named after Bellini's opera, or so Giovanni told her, pouring some wine for his aunt with a smile which nearly broke Kate's heart.

'And I believe that you know Lady St John?' asked Giovanni's mother.

Swallowing a mouthful of water nervously, Kate nodded. 'That's right. I decorated her house for her—and her London flat last year.'

Mrs Calverri nodded. 'She speaks very highly of you,' she said.

So Giovanni's mother had been talking to Lady St John, had she? Why on earth would she do that? Kate wondered. 'She told me that she'd met you when she was travelling around Europe,' she ventured.

'Indeed. Her father was at the embassy in Rome and my uncle was on the local staff there.' Mrs Calverri gave a smile that bordered on the wistful. 'Such a summer we girls had!'

Mr Calverri muttered something in Sicilian and his wife batted her eyelashes at him. 'Don't be jealous, *caro*. It was a long time ago!'

They ate cannoli for dessert—pastry tubes filled with fresh ricotta, bits of chocolate and candied fruit—and Michelina had left them with their coffee, when Giovanni's aunt Maria turned to her nephew.

'Will you show me your beautiful garden, Giovanni? It is so long since I have seen it.'

Kate looked nervously at Giovanni.

'Put some music on for Mama and Papa,' he said softly, and another pang of guilt hit him, hard, as he noted the anxiety which clouded her green eyes. What had he ever done for Kate, other than bring her unhappiness and loss? he asked himself in despair.

His aunt slipped her arm through his and they wandered outside, where the pale sunshine was warm on their skin.

The garden of the villa was beautiful and the pride of an old man who tended to it every day except Sunday and who had known Giovanni since he had been a baby.

Blue-green cypress trees pointed elegant spires skywards and lush, fleshy shrubs contrasted with the bright blooms of the semi-tropical flowers which spilled in such abundance on the edges of a perfect green lawn.

And in February the lawn was strewn with the white petals from the almond tree. 'Like confetti,' Giovanni had told Kate, and she had turned away from him, and he had guessed that the memory of her baby was still with her. And always would be with her, he thought now, his heart heavy.

Aunt Maria bent and fussed over the flowers, and pointed at the trees, and when they had reached the far end of the garden she stopped and spoke to him in Sicilian.

'Something is wrong, I think, Giovanni?'

His eyes narrowed. 'Wrong?'

'Something is troubling you,' said Aunt Maria perceptively. 'I can tell.'

His aunt was a wise and insightful woman, he thought, but he said nothing.

'Something which is threatening your happiness,' mused Aunt Maria, and she stooped to remove a dead flower.

'Happiness is too precarious not to be continually threatened,' he said quietly.

Aunt Maria straightened up, faded blue eyes, which must have once been just like his, narrowing as they regarded him.

'You and Anna were never right for one another, you know,' she said firmly. 'You are far too much your own man to be constrained by tradition. I told your father so. If you send a man to America at such a tender age, I said, you must be prepared for him to break against convention when he comes back.'

'I loved Anna,' he said, and his voice broke into a sigh. 'I never wanted to hurt her.'

'Of course you loved her!' declared his aunt passionately. 'But there is love, and there is love. Sometimes I thought you seemed more like brother and sister.' She regarded him thoughtfully. 'And a man like you needs real love; passionate love.'

'Oh, Zia Maria,' he said in a tone which was half-mocking.

The look she threw him back was equally mocking. 'You think that because I am of the older generation, that because I am old, I cannot understand passion?'

He shook his head, vigorously. '*Never!*' he declared fervently. 'Passion has no sell-by date.'

His aunt's eyes narrowed, and then she nodded thoughtfully. 'Sicilians are by nature and necessity the most secretive of people. Our culture and our history has always required our silence.'

'But not you?' queried Giovanni wryly. 'You're not like that?'

She laughed. 'No, you are right—I am not like that! My mother used to despair of my loose tongue!' She paused for a moment before she spoke. 'I think that your Kate means a very great deal to you?'

For a moment he didn't speak; he was not a man who unburdened his soul, nor one who bared his thoughts for others. And yet the weight of his guilt was an intolerably heavy one. He gave a heavy sigh.

'I think that, whatever my feelings for Kate, it may be too late for us now.'

Aunt Maria frowned. 'Too late? How can it be too late? Why is she here with you if it is, as you say, too late?'

A torrent of emotion seemed to well up like a tide inside him and his mouth twisted with pain.

'Tell me, Giovanni,' prompted his aunt softly. 'Tell me.'

There was a long, painful pause. 'She was having my baby!' he burst out at last. 'My *baby*, Zia Maria.'

Aunt Maria went very still. '*Was?*' she questioned quietly.

He nodded. 'I had only just found out. She told me, and I was...' His words tailed off.

'What were you, Giovanni?' she prompted quietly.

'I was so *angry*!' he bit out. 'Angry with her, and with myself—we had not planned a baby, you see!'

'That *is* the way these things sometimes go.' She smiled gently, but then her face grew serious. 'What happened?'

Could he bring himself to tell his aunt? To confess to his sin? 'I made love to her,' he said, in a cold, empty kind of voice. 'And within the hour she...she lost the baby.'

'And you blame yourself—is that it?'

'*Jesu*, Maria! Of course I blame myself!' he exploded. 'If I hadn't done that then she would still be pregnant!'

Aunt Maria shook her head. 'Oh, Giovanni, don't be ridiculous!' Her face was very candid as she laid a hand gently on his arm. 'Giovanni, think about this logically. Do you imagine that once a woman is pregnant, she and her partner never make love again until the baby arrives?'

'Of course not!'

'Well, then…what happened happened, and no one is to blame. It could well be,' she hesitated, 'that she would have lost the baby anyway. It would have occurred whether you made love to her or not. Sex does not cause miscarriages.'

'I've made her so unhappy!' he declared hotly.

'And yourself, by the look of you,' observed his aunt. 'The question you must ask yourself is whether you are going to let this ruin what you have between the two of you.'

And what *did* they have between them? He didn't know. He had never got around to asking her. Or telling her. He had been locked into a part-time relationship which was full of passion, but low on commitment. He had imagined that things would continue in their sweet, blissful way—but nothing ever remained the same, he realised now. Especially feelings. His own had changed somewhere along the way, but had hers?

'You must talk to her!' declared his aunt urgently. 'You must!'

'I know I must,' he echoed quietly.

The following morning he drove her into central Sicily, and Kate tried very hard to concentrate on the scenery and not the count-down happening inside her head as the hours before going home slowly ticked away. Tomorrow she would be on a flight back to England—her stay with Giovanni nothing but a bitter-sweet memory.

She had spent nights aching with the anticipation of how this moment might feel. She had imagined pain—a harsh, intense pain—but in that she had been wrong, because she felt numb. As if nothing could touch her. Please let me stay this way, she prayed, let me be strong when we say our goodbyes.

At least the scenery was spectacular enough to take her breath away as they drove up through the narrow, tortuous bends of the mountain roads. She saw forbidding rows of terracotta-roofed villages which seemed to hang in the air, and she shivered.

'They were built up there to keep out invaders from long ago,' mused Giovanni as he shot a glance at her frozen profile.

Kate thought that their very isolation and aloofness must be successful at discouraging modern-day tourists, too.

'Where are we going?' she asked.

'To Lake di Pergusa,' he said, and paused. 'The very spot where Persephone was abducted, all those years ago.'

Memories of the famous Sicilian myth came drifting back to her as he skirted the lake which was, rather disappointingly, skirted by a motor speedway. And the lake itself was noisy with waterskiers and motorboats.

He switched off the ignition, and they sat there for a moment or two in silence, while Kate's heart thudded with dread.

'So what do you think of my island, Kate?' he asked softly, wishing that she would look at him instead of presenting him with that unfathomable profile.

She tried hard not to imagine what this would be like if it was the beginning and not the end, but it took some doing. Resolutely, she kept her eyes fixed on the lake and tried to think what the old Kate would have said.

'Well, the circumstances of how I came to be here wouldn't have been my first choice,' she managed drily.

He recognised just what it must have cost her to say that, and his heart turned over. 'And are you recovered now?' he murmured. 'At least a little?'

*Until she recovers*. Like a bad dream, the words came back

to haunt her, but her heartbreak was her burden to carry, not his.

She nodded. 'More than a little. You see—I barely had time to realise I was pregnant, before…' Her voice wobbled, and she took a deep breath before she spoke again. 'Maybe that helped a bit.'

He felt the knife-twist of bitter regret. 'I wish I could undo the past, Kate.'

She turned to him then and her green eyes were huge in her face. Her words came out on a tremble. 'What, all of it?' Was he saying that he wished he had never met her, was that it?

He shook his head. Had she misunderstood him so badly, or had his actions caused her to do so? 'The bad bits—the times when I was angry, when I spoke so harshly to you.' His eyes imprisoned hers with their blue fire.

Something akin to hope flared in her heart, and, no matter how hard she tried to quash it, it stubbornly refused to die. 'And the good bits?' she asked tremulously. 'What of those?'

He had spent a lifetime keeping his feelings hidden, locked away inside his secret Sicilian nature, but suddenly he found himself wanting to tell her—*needing* to tell her. 'I would relive them over and over and over again,' he said softly. 'The very first time I saw you, what I felt for you—'

'Lust,' she forced herself to say, and bit her lip.

He saw the uncertainty on her face and shook his head. 'Passion,' he corrected gently. 'Not lust, *cara*, but passion. Something which had never entered my life before I met you.'

'Not even with Anna?' The words were out before she could stop them.

'Not even with Anna.' He sighed, knowing that he owed her everything, but the most important thing of all was the truth. Even if she did not want him, he owed her that.

'Anna and I had all the right ingredients for a relationship.

We had mutual liking and respect, and we both wanted a perfect marriage, I guess.' He shrugged. 'But life doesn't always conform to the ideals you set yourself. The moment I met you, my subconscious must have been telling me that there are emotions which go beyond reason, beyond understanding, even.'

Her heart began to thud. 'And what emotions are they?' she questioned painfully.

There was a long pause, and his blue eyes were luminous as he looked at her. 'Why, love, of course, *cara mia*. Just love.'

Just love? *Just* love? She stared at him, her heart not daring to believe the words he had just said to her.

'I love you, Kate. *Ti vogghiu beni*. I want you and I need you…by my side, and in my heart. Forever.'

'Oh, Giovanni.' Words she had longed for, prayed for. Tears began to slide down her cheeks. 'Giovanni,' she said brokenly.

'Don't cry, *cara mia*,' he beseeched. 'Why are you crying?'

'Because…' She thought of his honesty and at last allowed her own true feelings to come flooding out, like a river which had burst its banks. 'Because I thought you didn't want me any more—'

'Not *want* you?' he demanded incredulously. 'Not *want* you?'

'You haven't come near me since…'

'Since the baby?' he prompted painfully, his mouth twisting. 'You want to know why? Because I blamed myself! If I hadn't made love to you—'

'But it could have happened anyway!' she told him fiercely.

'I know that. Now.'

Tenderly he wiped the tears from her cheek and she looked up into his face. 'You d-do?'

He nodded. 'My aunt Maria helped me see things in perspective.'

'You told her?' asked Kate in surprise.

His eyes narrowed. 'You don't mind?'

How could she mind about something that had absolved his guilt? It was just the thought of her aloof Giovanni confiding in something as personal as that to his aunt!

He saw her look of confusion.

'Aunt Maria realised that I was hurting,' he told her. 'And she also realised that what you and I had between us was strong—much too strong to be broken. She made me realise that some things happen just because they are meant to. That men have been making love to pregnant women since time began—and there was no earthly reason why we shouldn't have done the same.'

'I shouldn't have let you shoulder the burden of guilt,' she told him falteringly. 'But I was hurting too much to be able to reach out and help you—and you seemed so proud and remote. You wouldn't come near me afterwards—you wouldn't even touch me.'

'I thought that you would push me away,' he admitted. 'As well as feeling I didn't deserve to touch you.'

Kate shook her head wonderingly. 'And I thought that you just didn't want my help. Or my body.'

He gave her a searingly honest look of total capitulation. 'I want everything you're prepared to give me,' he said simply.

'Then you'd better have my love, Giovanni—because it's yours.' Her voice trembled with emotion. 'Only yours.'

He was filled with the urgent need to kiss her, but he wanted to vanquish all the remaining shadows that lingered between them.

'Does it still hurt?' he asked in a low voice. 'About the baby?'

She nodded. The truth was painful, yes, but out of pain

grew healing, and a new kind of maturity. 'A little. But it gets easier day by day.'

'I want to give you more babies,' he whispered. 'As many as you want. And I want to marry you. *Mi vo spusari, cara?*'

She didn't need to speak fluent Sicilian to understand what he had just said. '*Sí, caro. Sí.*' Her eyes grew misty as she gently ran her fingertips lovingly around the hard, proud line of his jaw, just as she had been longing to for days and days.

'Now kiss me, please,' she said shakily, and he took her in his arms and held her for a long, restoring moment and then did exactly that.

# EPILOGUE

THE lusty cries had abated at last, and Kate slanted Giovanni a rueful smile as she sank down onto the sofa next to him.

'He has lungs, our baby!' she murmured.

'He will sing opera one day,' predicted Giovanni with the kind of expansive pride he always used when talking about his son.

'I thought he was going into parliament?' teased Kate.

'Maybe.' He reached his arm out and pulled her close to him, absently and tenderly kissing the top of her head. 'Shall I make dinner now?' he murmured.

'Oh, if only your mother could hear you say that!' she giggled. 'She once told me that you had never set foot inside the kitchen in your life!'

'Ah, but that was before I married my independent Kate who taught me everything I know. Well, *nearly* everything!' His blue eyes glittered as he planted another kiss on top of her fragrant red hair.

'Two years ago tomorrow we've been married,' she said wonderingly. 'Can you believe it?'

Two years? They might as well have been two minutes, they had swept by with such sweet, glorious abandon. A wife, and now a son. Giovanni closed his eyes. Contentment and passion—an unbeatable combination, and one which seemed just as easy as breathing, such was his life with Kate.

Their time together had not been completely without some tensions—but then life was never like that. During the early stages of her pregnancy, he had treated her as he would have a delicate piece of porcelain, and Kate had not objected, not once. As each week had passed, they had breathed sighs of

183

relief that the baby was growing safely, and as her body had burgeoned with the new life, so had their love for each other. Deeper and deeper, so that some mornings she had felt she really ought to pinch herself.

The wedding had been in London and afterwards there had been a big post-wedding party in Sicily for all Giovanni's family and friends. Kate had met Anna for the first time, then already pregnant by Guido. She and Giovanni's brother had been married the previous summer, and their happiness was evident for all to see.

Anna had sought Kate out in what had proved initially to be a rather nervous meeting on both sides, but all bitterness had been forgotten when her new sister-in-law had admired Kate's wedding band.

'It's very beautiful,' she had said. 'I understand that Giovanni designed it?'

'Yes.' Kate's smile had faltered, knowing that she must say something about the past. 'Anna, listen, I'm sorry—'

'No!' The dark-haired beauty had shaken her smooth head firmly. 'It is all in the past and the only memories I have of Giovanni are good ones. I am happier now than I could have ever been with him; I realise that now. Guido,' she had added, with a slow, luminous smile, 'he is the right man for me—and I am the right woman for him.'

Guido and Anna were installed in their home in the hills outside Palermo, Guido having taken over the running of the factory, whilst Giovanni now masterminded the international side of the business from his brand-new offices in central London.

He and Kate had decided not to settle in Sicily—the dramatic change in culture would not have suited his wife, he had decided. Nor him. His aunt had been right—his trip to America had made him truly cosmopolitan—although in his heart he would always be a Sicilian.

Instead, he and Kate would spend as many holidays as

possible in his homeland, and especially in springtime, which held such tender memories for them both.

'Kate?'

She turned her head up to look at him lazily, basking as always in the glow of love from his eyes. 'Mmm?'

'Do you want your anniversary present now?'

'Shouldn't I wait?'

'Have one today, and something else tomorrow,' he said, smiling as he remembered the glittering diamond cross which lay in a small box in his sock drawer. 'Look over there.'

She followed the direction of his gaze to a low table that stood in the window of their airy town-house and saw a small box standing next to the fruit bowl. Why hadn't she noticed it before?

She walked over and picked it up, and turned to face him, a soft smile curving her lips. 'You buy me too many presents,' she protested, but only halfheartedly.

He shook his head, admiring the way her silk skirt clung to the slim swell of her bottom. His beautiful Kate! 'Never enough,' he murmured indulgently.

She flipped the box open, and inside was a ring—a circlet of bright, glittering diamonds—and she stared at him. 'Oh, darling,' she whispered. 'It's exquisite.'

'Come over here,' he instructed throatily. 'And let me put it on.'

She walked towards him, almost dazzled by the blaze of love from his eyes, perching next to him on the sofa, aware of the warm male scent of him, and of how much she wanted him. Always wanted him.

He slipped the ring onto her finger above the plain wedding band she wore and it fitted perfectly, as she had known it would.

There had been no engagement ring—they had both quietly decided that to have one would be disrespectful to Anna.

'It's an eternity ring,' he told her softly. 'It means that you are mine for all eternity, *cara*—as I am yours.'

She sighed with pleasure. 'Oh, Giovanni, you say the most beautiful things—promise me you'll never stop saying them!'

'Never!' He smiled as he watched her hold her hand up to the light and the ring threw off rainbow rays. 'The first time I saw you I wanted to see you in diamonds,' he admitted.

It was like a fairy story she could never hear too often. 'What else?' she questioned throatily.

'I wondered if you wore silk next to your skin.' His voice was husky now and his eyes alight with promise as they lazily scanned her body with proprietorial air. 'And now I know that you do.'

'Mmm.' The promise in his eyes was reflected in her own. 'And do you know what I thought the first time I saw you?'

He loved this game. 'What?'

She gave him a smile which was pure provocation. 'How much I'd like you to undress me.'

His eyes glittered. 'Did you?'

'Mmm.'

'Then I think I'd better fulfil your every wish, don't you, *cara*?' he murmured, and pulled her into his arms.

**Modern Romance**™
...seduction and
passion guaranteed

**Tender Romance**™
...love affairs that
last a lifetime

**Sensual Romance**™
...sassy, sexy and
seductive

*Blaze*
...sultry days and
steamy nights

**Medical Romance**™
...medical drama on
the pulse

**Historical Romance**™
...rich, vivid and
passionate

*29 new titles every month.*

*With all kinds of Romance for
every kind of mood...*

MILLS & BOON®

*Makes any time special*™

MAT4

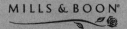

MILLS & BOON®

# Modern Romance™

**RAFAELLO'S MISTRESS** *by Lynne Graham*

Glory's fantasies became reality when she enjoyed a passionate affair with Rafaello Grazzini—but his father used blackmail to bring their fairytale to an end. Years later Glory begs Rafaello for help. He agrees on one condition – that she become his mistress…

**THE BELLINI BRIDE** *by Michelle Reid*

Marco Bellini had it all: success, wealth, and Antonia – the woman who'd shared his bed for a year. Marco had to marry and produce an heir and Antonia's past rendered her unsuitable as a Bellini bride – but Marco knew she was the only woman he wanted…

**SLEEPING PARTNERS** *by Helen Brooks*

Powerful tycoon Clay Lincoln was the only man who could save Robyn's business. Years ago, Clay had rejected her, but now he was clearly impressed by the woman she had become – and wanted to be her sleeping partner in more than one sense!

**THE MILLIONAIRE'S MARRIAGE** *by Catherine Spencer*

Max Logan was convinced Gabriella had trapped him into marriage for his millions. As far as he was concerned they were finished! But then they were forced to act happily married for two weeks – and that meant sharing a bed! Was this her chance to prove to Max that she'd married for love?

## On sale 2nd November 2001

*Available at most branches of WH Smith, Tesco, Martins, Borders, Eason, Sainsbury's, Woolworths and most good paperback bookshops.*

1001/01a

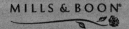

# 4 FREE

## books and a surprise gift!

We would like to take this opportunity to thank you for reading this Mills & Boon® book by offering you the chance to take FOUR more specially selected titles from the Modern Romance™ series absolutely FREE! We're also making this offer to introduce you to the benefits of the Reader Service™—

★ FREE home delivery
★ FREE gifts and competitions
★ FREE monthly Newsletter
★ Exclusive Reader Service discounts
★ Books available before they're in the shops

Accepting these FREE books and gift places you under no obligation to buy, you may cancel at any time, even after receiving your free shipment. Simply complete your details below and return the entire page to the address below. *You don't even need a stamp!*

**YES!** Please send me 4 free Modern Romance books and a surprise gift. I understand that unless you hear from me, I will receive 6 superb new titles every month for just £2.49 each, postage and packing free. I am under no obligation to purchase any books and may cancel my subscription at any time. The free books and gift will be mine to keep in any case.

P1ZEA

Ms/Mrs/Miss/Mr .............................Initials......................................
BLOCK CAPITALS PLEASE

Surname ....................................................................................................

Address ....................................................................................................

..................................................................................................................

.............................................................Postcode.................................

**Send this whole page to:**
**UK: FREEPOST CN81, Croydon, CR9 3WZ**
**EIRE: PO Box 4546, Kilcock, County Kildare (stamp required)**